P

# *Riverman*

'Been very bad, hasn't it?' Jean sounded flat. She looked at Tim with heavy eyes.

Tim shrugged.

'Larry's going back up the river . . . He can take you . . . I think you should go.'

Tim has always been known as the 'Shrimp', and in the rugged mining town of Zeehan, a four-foot-nothing kid is of no use to anyone. But the Tasmanian mine disaster of 1912 tragically changes all that for ever, and Tim finds himself beginning a dangerous and exciting adventure as he sets off with his uncle on a journey he'll never forget.

*Riverman* was winner of the 1988 IBBY Honour Diploma (Australia) and was shortlisted for the 1987 Australian Children's Book of the Year Award and the 1987 Guardian Children's Fiction Award.

Also by Allan Baillie

*Adrift*
*Little Brother*
*Eagle Island*
*Megan's Star*
*Hero*
*Mates*
*The China Coin*
*Little Monster*

**Picture Books**

*Drac and the Gremlin*
*Bawshou Rescues the Sun*
(with Chun-Chan Yeh)
*The Boss*

# *Riverman*

## Allan Baillie

**Puffin Books**

Puffin Books
Penguin Books Australia Ltd
487 Maroondah Highway, PO Box 257
Ringwood, Victoria 3134, Australia
Penguin Books Ltd
Harmondsworth, Middlesex, England
Viking Penguin, A Division of Penguin Books USA Inc.
375 Hudson Street, New York, New York 10014, USA
Penguin Books Canada Limited
10 Alcorn Avenue, Toronto, Ontario, Canada M4V 1E4
Penguin Books (N.Z.) Ltd
182-190 Wairau Road, Auckland 10, New Zealand

First published by Blackie and Son Limited, 1986
First published in Australia in 1986 by Thomas Nelson Australia
First published in Puffin, 1992
10 9 8 7 6 5 4 3 2 1
Copyright © Allan Baillie, 1986

Offset from the Nelson hardback edition

Made and printed in Australia by Australian Print Group

National Library of Australia
Cataloguing-in-Publication data:

Baillie, Allan, 1943-
Riverman.
ISBN 0 14 034193 5.
I. Title
A823.3

# Contents

My deep thanks to the people of Queenstown, Zeehan and Strahan who helped with *Riverman*. Especially Les Brown of Zeehan, Norm Riggs of Queenstown, Harry McDermott of Strahan and Reg Morrison of Strahan for their memories and advice.

Research for *Riverman* was assisted by a Special Purpose Grant from the Australia Council.

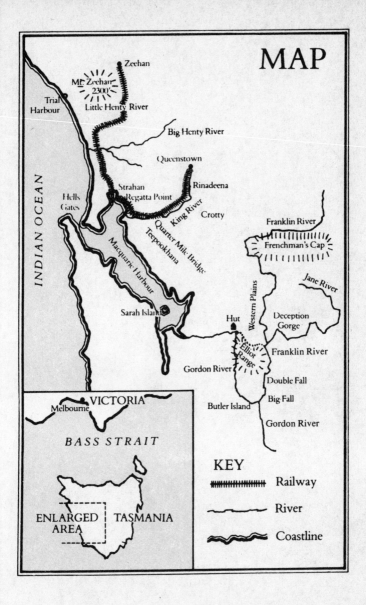

# MAP

Zeehan

Mt. Zeehan 2300'

Trial Harbour

Little Henty River

Big Henty River

Queenstown

INDIAN OCEAN

Hells Gates

Strahan
Regatta Point

Rinadeena

King River

Crotty

Quarter Mile Bridge

Teepookhana

Macquarie Harbour

Franklin River

Frenchman's Cap

Jane River

Sarah Island

Hut

Western Plains

Deception Gorge

Elliot Range

Franklin River

Gordon River

Double Fall

Butler Island

Big Fall

Gordon River

Melbourne

VICTORIA

BASS STRAIT

ENLARGED AREA

TASMANIA

## KEY

|  |  |
|---|---|
| ▪▪▪▪▪▪▪▪▪ | Railway |
| ⌒⌒⌒ | River |
| ≈≈≈ | Coastline |

# The Gift

'Anyhow, I've got a gift for you,' said the little old man as he shrugged into a boy's parka.

'A knife?' Brian Walker stopped trying to jam his huge feet into men's boots and looked around at the piled confusion of the campers' shop.

'Better than that. Maybe it's the best thing you'll ever see.' The little old man laughed. 'Or maybe it's just a pain in the neck.'

That was just like Tim Walker—a bundle of puzzles. Brian had only asked his dad about the Walker family history for a school project, and now here he was two thousand kilometres from his Sydney home with an old man who was as mad as a parrot. Dear old Dad had said: 'You want to write to your Great Uncle Tim, that's what you want to do.'

So Brian had written to Great Uncle Tim in Hobart: 'Can you please tell me what our family did in the old days?'

And Great Uncle Tim had written back: 'No. But I can show you. Come on down, and see.' With an airline ticket in the envelope.

And the puzzles had begun.

Dad told Brian that Great Uncle Tim had been a pioneer in the wild west of Tasmania when there were no roads and great areas of the map were blank; that he had saved the life of Great Grandad Larry, built like a train, in the

9

heart of the wilderness when he was only twelve. Brian had naturally expected Great Uncle Tim to be, well, great.

But Great Uncle Tim was a shrimp, a leprechaun, a gnome. He was no bigger than a ten-year-old boy and he moved and smiled like one. Brian had to keep on noting the fine lines around the eyes and mouth to remind him that Great Uncle Tim was well over eighty.

Asking Tim about his life in the wilds was like chasing a rainbow with a butterfly net. He mentioned things like cannibal country, chasing pirates, being attacked by a tiger . . . you *knew* he was just dropping a line, but you couldn't be really, positively, sure.

So he keeps on saying these crazy things and you have to keep on asking what they mean. It does no good at all, but you have to keep on trying.

'What is the gift, Uncle?' Brian said.

'You'll have to see it,' Great Uncle Tim said, as he led the way out of the campers' shop. 'You might say it's why I wanted you to come here.'

Brian sighed.

'It's a long way to go.'

Next day they left Hobart in a light plane to cross great humped ranges, mysterious valleys stroked by fingers of mist, dark forests and a shining inland sea. They landed at the edge of the scarred and bare orange hills of Queenstown and wandered around the town in a rented car.

Uncle Tim nodded at the sky over an ugly hill. 'Used to be a mountain of earth, rock and copper there. And a mine and a god-awful disaster.'

'What happened?'

Uncle Tim shook his head. 'Tell you later.' He walked away.

They stopped before a carefully-restored green locomotive caught climbing an impossible slope, as if it was aiming at the moon.

'Trains can't go up a hill like that,' said Brian.

10

Uncle Tim smiled warmly at the locomotive and said: 'This is *Number Three*—and it did. Once, just once, it just about flew. I was there, in the cabin—we were all scared blind, but we couldn't stop.'

★ ★ ★

They left Queenstown the next morning, turned from the road and passed a guarded barrier. They weaved around motionless road-building machines and drove along a lonely track, winding over mountains and into dense forest.

'They were going to build a dam and I was pretty nervous about—about the gift,' Uncle Tim said. 'They've stopped it now, but I got thinking.'

He parked the car at a deserted truck base and Brian stamped into his boots, wriggled into a bright yellow parka, settled a heavy pack on his back.

'I mean, I've been worrying about it for more than seventy years. Trying to look after it with blokes tipping forests into the river.' Uncle Tim sloshed quickly along an abandoned dam road until it became a river of mud, then turned into the forest. 'It's about time I passed it on.'

For the rest of the day he led Brian into a silent forest of dripping trees, moss and ferns. He pushed tirelessly against tangled vines, fallen branches and thorns. At one stage he rolled over the thorns, rather than trying to walk through them. He often stopped and waited for Brian to catch up.

Uncle Tim finally came to a halt at a small level space overlooking a racing river and massive green mountains.

'That's the Franklin river. Me, a man called Straw and your Great Grandad Larry came *up* that wild river in 1912, tackling killer trees and runaway rivers—ah, we were all a little mad.'

'That was when you saved Great Grandad Larry?'

'Who told you that? Oh, yes, just round a bend or two,

11

it started. But he saved me too. It was all a matter of size.'

'Size?'

'He was as big as you're going to be. If I had been as big as you or he'd been as little as me, I wouldn't be here to tell you about the tree—and you wouldn't be here to listen.'

'Oh.' Brian was confused.

'And that's your gift, down that slope. You can see the top.'

Brian pushed through some scrub and stopped as the ground fell away before him. Before and below him he could see about six grand old pines, creaking in a tumbling wave of darker trees. Between the trunks of the pines were strewn black branches and the long-dead trunks of other trees.

Brian was disappointed. 'Those trees, then?'

Uncle Tim smiled down at the six trees. 'Not *those* trees, Brian. *That* single tree. It is only one tree.'

Brian squinted at the trees again and began to see into the shadows. The dead trunks were not lying on the forest floor but in a cradle formed by the six pines. Below the dead trunks of the six pines ran together into a single massive base.

'Just one tree?'

'Yup. The people who know about it call it Walker's Tree. It's ours. Yours.'

Brian stood beside the little man and frowned down at the top of his head. 'But what do I do with it?'

Uncle Tim squatted on the edge of the cliff and bent a twig. 'Well, it's not a Christmas present, like a bicycle,' he admitted. 'You might not want any part of it. But let me tell you the story first . . . .'

# The Mine

# 1
# Silver City

'Fire!'

Tim opened an eye at the low call. He sniffed quickly, but there was nothing in the air.

Someone was running past the house, calling so softly that his voice barely carried over the sound of his pounding boots.

Tim sat up and heard the frantic ringing of a distant bell. He rolled silently from his flour-bag bed to avoid waking his baby brother, and vaulted through the window. He was already dressed, a frayed shirt, a black guernsey and shorts cut back from his father's old trousers, grey braces and bare feet. He had gone to bed like this for weeks to make sure he didn't miss the next fire.

A scrawny shadow was jerking down the moon-washed street. Tim splashed after the runner, identifying him by the sound of the boots his parents forced him to wear. Tim slid up to the tall boy as he nervously skirted a pair of large puddles—the misery of owning boots is that you have to clean them.

'Arr there, Ben, what's it?' Tim said out the side of his mouth.

The wild bell stopped and was replaced by a single loud clang, meaning the fire was in the east of town, near the railway station. They were running that way already.

'Fire!' called Ben, for the boys still in bed. 'Oh, Walker. Probably only a house.' And Ben seemed to accelerate.

Tim heard the slight annoyance in Ben's voice but ignored it. Ben was about the only boy in town who didn't call Tim 'Shrimp', and you have to take small favours where you find them.

'Better than nothing,' Tim said, and grinned up at Ben.

Ben sighed and ran ahead, past an abandoned silver-lead mine, still smelling of wet wood and rusting iron, along a dark curved street flanked by huddled wooden houses and towards the warm glow of bright yellow light. The bell went mad again as Tim stumbled after Ben into the din of the dazzling heart of Zeehan, Silver City of 1912.

Tim was quite sure that this was the centre of the world. Only a few years ago, they said, the flat valley was nothing but grass and straggly bush. Then a prospector struck silver. Mining companies shouldered each other aside in a desperate rush for rich ore, and tents became a street of wooden buildings, became a village, a town, a city!

Now the new electric light blazed from tall poles, making Zeehan as modern as London and New York. The brass trumpets and drums of the Zeehan Military Band were happily blasting the glittering Gaiety Theatre as if they were trying to bring the walls down before the night's movie show. Further down Main Street deaf old Steve Dodd, in his gleaming livery, was cantering his four proud horses and coach past the band like an emperor on parade. Oh, it was a great night!

But Ben ran into trouble. He was striding along the steam tramway on the side of the street, where trucks of silver-lead ore rolled from the mines round the town to the station during the day, when he cannoned into a miner. Tim staggered to a stop in alarm, realizing that Ben could not have picked a worse place to butt a man.

They were outside the 'Blood House', the Exchange, the toughest of the fifteen hotels jammed together on this single street. So tough they called Saturday night 'Fight

Night' because of the brawling, and more miners were now spilling through the doors.

The rammed miner picked Ben from the road by his neck, glared at him blackly and drew back his fist.

'You gonna see the fire, Mr Paley?' Tim called quickly.

'What?' The miner, a man built like a small elephant, blinked and lowered his fist a fraction. He seemed to be trying to think. 'Ah . . . you're Jean's kid—'

'Yes.' Tim's mum worked as a cleaner in the Exchange and most of the miners knew Tim.

'We're going to see the fire. Sorry we hurt you.'

The miner opened his fist. 'Hurt me? You little fleas?' He roared with laughter.

'Outertheway!'

Tim leapt sideways and the miner dropped Ben in surprise as the other miners cheered.

Two men in loose shirts and floppy hats ran like horses, holding a wooden bar which pulled a big-wheeled box with a mass of canvas hose wrapped round it. Behind them two horses tried to gallop as they hauled a large cart full of drums of water, swinging stirrup pumps and men. One man clung to the cart as he struggled to get his arm into a flapping shirt sleeve.

The Zeehan Fire Brigade clanged, rattled and careered towards the fire and deaf Steve Dodd's carriage.

Tim pulled Ben to his feet as Dodd's horses reared in fright at the sound behind them. Dodd shouted at the horses as the carriage careered across the street and the charge of the fire brigade became a confused retreat. The big-wheeled box was dropped before the water cart as firemen bolted clear of the snorting horses.

'C'mon, we can beat them!' shouted Tim. He ran down a lane as the carriage slammed against the water cart, the fire horses hissed steam at Dodd's horses and Dodd flicked his whip at the firemen in fury. It would take a while to untangle the traffic jam.

Tim jogged towards the railway station, the only way

17

in or out of Zeehan, until he saw a red haze above the corrugated iron roofs to his left. Not too far now, maybe no more than a quarter mile.

He slowed his run to a walk as he neared the fire and the crowd, groups of men and women standing before the blaze and clusters of boys watching furtively from the shadows.

'Well—' Ben sounded uncomfortable. 'We're here.'

'And we beat the fire brigade. By miles,' Tim grinned.

'Thought that bloke was going to knock me into next Friday. Hell, that was close.'

'Ah, it wasn't that bad—' Tim smiled modestly.

'Dunno what would've happened if the fire brigade hadn't come by. Well, see ya.' And Ben shuffled quickly away to join a few boys his own size.

Tim watched him go with the smile dying on his face; then he shrugged and turned to the fire. After all, he was used to it. A four foot nothing kid is really not much good to anyone. In a footy game, or even cricket, he was only picked for the teams after the girls—and the rest of the time he was allowed to tag along if it absolutely couldn't be helped. Tonight it could be helped.

'Not bad,' Tim said, as if he was talking to someone, an art he had developed while wandering alone on Mount Zeehan.

A one-chimney house was now a roaring bonfire. The pine walls were crackling in the heat and, as he watched, a glass window exploded. Flames were rising ten feet above the roof, throwing a strange moving light across the faces of the crowd.

'But hotels are always better.'

Tim's first memory of the Silver City was of standing beside Dad, watching the Zeehan Hotel burst into flame. The hotels of Zeehan had been built hastily for the miners, mostly of pine with their walls lined with scrim—hessian—and covered with paper. Like the houses they all had their own water tanks because there was no town

18

water supply. Tim had seen a shop beside the Zeehan Hotel ignite from the hotel fire, then another shop, and another until the Palace Hotel joined the blaze. Since then there had been so many fires Tim couldn't count them.

'Here's the cavalry—' said Tim.

The firemen arrived in a bustle. A stirrup pump was made fast to one end of the hose with a slam and a spin, plunged into a drum, the lever worked by two red-faced men and the hose began to spurt water at the house. Someone cheered, but it was a vain effort.

'It's gone,' Tim said. But he knew the house and it had been derelict for months. Funny how many of the fires were in empty houses now. Tim thought there were maybe a hundred houses in Zeehan where the people who had lived there had just packed and left.

The roof of the house sagged and crashed through the inner walls in a shower of sparks. The firemen gave up trying to save the house and turned their hose on the neighbouring houses to stop the fire spreading. People were laughing and shouting encouragement to them as if they were at a barbecue. Tim yelled and clapped.

"Allo, 'allo, what have we here?'

Tim stopped in mid-yell. For an instant he thought of bolting, but the voice was too close. He tried a cool smile, gave it the touch of a sneer and turned. 'Hello Henry. Did ya get lost?'

Henry Coutts. Of course he had to be here. You could rely on Henry *never* to let you feel lonely. Almost like a mate, was Henry.

A heavy youth with his thumbs in his braces leered at Tim from a group of lumpy boys who seemed to live in his shadow.

'I don't get lost, Shrimp. Ever. What're you doing in my stretch? Don'tya know it's dangerous out here?'

'Just lookin' round. Anyway, who said you own this place?'

'I say who comes to this fire and who doesn't.'

19

'Why?'

'It's my fire.'

Tim blinked. '*Your* fire?'

Coutts looked nervously over his shoulder. 'Shut up!' he hissed and hit Tim in the stomach.

Tim felt like a burst paper bag. He hung limply over Coutts' arm, then toppled slowly to the mud. He couldn't move a leg or an arm to save himself. He hit the ground with the side of his head and someone screwed his head into the mud, half-filling his gasping mouth with slime. For a while everyone was laughing; then his head was dropped in the mud and the laughter stopped.

Tim sensed someone crouched near his head while he fought to breathe, straining his ribs to fill his lungs. But the figure did not move or say anything until the air stopped sighing through Tim's lips and he could wipe his face and see again.

'How's it going?' A man built like a short stone column with thick black arms reached for Tim's shoulder.

'Dad?' Tim's voice wavered. Dad could not be here, he was working the 'nana' carts, the ore carts, at the smelters.

'Can you stand up?' Light played across the man's face, catching the old square spectacles, the cropped, grey-speckled hair, the light scar across his right cheekbone, the easy smile lines around his mouth.

It *was* Dad. Tim nodded and leaned into the man's steady rising hand. He looked briefly about him as he steadied on his feet. The firemen were still hosing the rim of the fire, but Coutts and his gang were gone. Tim began to feel the comfortable warmth of anger, but there was something terribly wrong.

Tim turned to Dad. 'How come—' he winced, 'how come you're here? Not at the smelter?'

Dad sighed. 'You're going to have to give up being a boy. Again.'

# 2

# The Thunderer

'Oh.'

Tim understood. He watched the single front wall sag and keel over with a crash.

'The smelter let me go,' Dad said flatly.

Tim nodded. In his twelve years he had been with Dad for a total of five. For most of the rest he had had to try to take Dad's place around the house.

'You're leaving again, then?'

'You know how it is.'

'Ah, yeah.'

Dad would land mining jobs for a few months, then there would be a strike and he would have to leave the area, or the mine would run out of metal or flood and close down. Then Dad would chop trees with his brother, or carry stores to remote outposts on horseback until other mines opened. He had worked for the smelters for almost a year but the family all knew the end was coming. Jobs in the west just did not last.

'Anyway, I got a present for you.' Dad opened his hessian bag on the mud and pulled a hunk of wood from it.

Tim took it from Dad's hands and staggered a little under the weight. It was the size of a pumpkin. 'White pine?'

Dad nodded. 'Real Huon pine. A bloke was making

fence posts from it. Thought you might like to do some whittling. Let's go home.'

Tim held the wood up to the light of the flame, then tucked it safely under his arm. 'Thanks Dad, that's beaut.'

They walked from the fire.

Dad shrugged. 'Why do I always find you fighting giants?'

'Sorry, Dad. There's just nobody my size. They're *all* giants.'

Dad thought for a moment; then he laughed and scrabbled his fingers through his son's basin-cropped hair. 'Then you've just got to run like hell.'

'I was going to when he hit me.'

'The idea is to run like hell *before* he hits you.' The man slung a sooty arm over Tim's shoulder. For a time Dad didn't mention the smelters. Tim forgot the pain in his stomach and they talked about school and fishing like old mates. But as they wandered up Main Street and turned into their dimly-lit corner of the town, Tim just stopped talking. He was looking into the loneliness of next week.

Dad looked sideways and understood. 'Maybe I won't be so long away this time.'

Tim shrugged.

'And when I come back, we'll make up for it, eh?' Dad squeezed Tim's shoulder. 'What about the time we dammed that creek for a swimming hole, or hunted mutton birds around Trial Harbour, or climbed Mount Zeehan, or found that wreck in the surf—'

'It's all right,' said Tim slowly. 'When you're here.'

They reached home in an awkward silence. The house loomed out of the shadows, solid tongue-and-groove walls supporting a small shingle roof and a chimney scraping against an old water tank. Even the building looked desolate.

But Dad walked round the house to a square of bright light spilling over the vegetable garden and opened the back door into the kitchen. 'We need a bath,' he said, then: 'Nipper!'

A huge bearded man was sitting at the scrubbed pine table with Mum. For a moment he was a stranger to Tim, but Dad whooped and hauled him to his feet as if he was a stuffed bear.

Mum—or Jean—looked up at Dad in a surprise touched with pain. A long while ago, maybe when Tim began cooking meals while Mum was working at the hotel, Tim stopped calling his mother 'Mum'. Or at least while Dad was away. During those long, bleak periods he called her 'Jean', somehow making them into a special team facing the world. Funny, but when Jean was Mum, she was an angular woman with plain dark-brown hair pulled back into a bun, a thin nose, hard lips and a glint in her eye. Yet when Mum was Jean, wisps of her hair drifted across her forehead, caught the sun and turned gold. Her brown eyes were shot with flecks of green, her lips hid a secret joke and Tim could see past the lines in her face the hint of wild little girl she had once been. Mum was strong and just, but Jean was fun.

'How's it going, Bert?' the huge man—Larry—said. 'How d'you like the whiskers?'

Larry was Tim's only uncle, but Tim had stopped calling him 'Uncle' since his tenth birthday. He simply called him 'Larry' when he saw him and they were both happy with that. Larry spent most of his time chopping down trees on wild rivers in the rain forest and dropped in on Dad for a few weeks a year to 'dry out'. He must have arrived in Zeehan tonight.

'Even more like a gorilla. They'll put you in a cage.'

'Keeps my jaw warm.'

'What've you been up to?' Jean said to Tim.

Tim placed the block on the table while he thought of an answer.

Larry raised a finger the size of a cigar and poked it at Tim. 'Been watching fires, eh?'

23

'I thought you were in bed,' Jean said. 'You should have been in bed.'

'How'd you get that mud all over you?' Larry levered himself from the chair. He seemed to keep on growing long after he had stood up.

'Get him in a bath and we'll tell you all about it,' Dad said.

Jean looked at Tim in annoyance, but she carried a large galvanized iron tub out of the back door and turned the tank tap on full over it.

'Get outa the clothes, Tim.' Dad pinched at the muddy guernsey.

Jean staggered back into the kitchen, leaning back from the quarter-full tub and holding the door open with her knee.

Larry stoked the stove. 'Get into a fight?'

Tim nodded. He had struggled out of his guernsey, thrown off his braces and was burying his head in his sodden blouse. He was trying to pretend that Larry was not here, so he could have a bath without feeling embarrassed. Jean was all right, or at least tolerable, because she was always there, but Larry was still a stranger.

Jean placed a slab of soap and a scrubbing brush by the tub, now on the floor, and filled the tub with water from the great kettle from the stove. She went outside again to fill the kettle.

'What happened?' Larry passed Dad a mug of tea.

'Coutts hit me.' Tim undid the buttons of his blue serge shorts and wondered how fast he could move into the tub. The shorts had once been Dad's work trousers, but Jean had cut them to above Tim's knees and built them around the fly to fit Tim almost perfectly. But now they were too tight, too wet to take off fast enough. He lowered them to his knees and began to stagger backwards towards the steaming tub.

24

Larry laughed and caught his arm. 'This Coutts boy? How many times he hit you?'

Tim looked at Dad sipping his tea. 'Once,' he muttered, and kicked away the shorts. He stepped quickly to the tub and almost dropped into the water. He opened his mouth at the shock of the very warm water.

'Once?' Larry said loudly. 'Only once?' He turned from Tim and forgot about him for most of the evening.

Which was fine by Tim. He could soak himself in the lovely hot water, hide himself in the steam and pretend Larry wasn't there. Tim could not think of this hard-faced giant from the wilds as an uncle and Larry probably only thought of Tim as 'Bert's brat' rather than as anything important, like a nephew.

Tim reached up to the table, took the Huon block from the table and soaked it until the dark veins traced elaborate etchings through the wood, telling him what he could do with it. For a boy with a knife it was very good gift.

Jean slammed the great kettle on the stove and wiped her hands on her apron. She turned to Dad with a tightness about her face. 'You're home early.'

Dad took her hand. 'They put me off.'

'Well—' Jean shrugged.

'At least we could see it coming.'

Tim didn't want to hear any more. He knew where it would lead. He scrubbed noisily.

Perhaps Jean didn't want to hear it either. She changed the subject. 'Where'd you find Tim?'

'Ah, there was a fire near the station. Had a look and he was there.'

'Oh.' Jean's tone meant future trouble.

'It was a pretty good fire,' Tim said quickly. 'Flames hundreds of feet high. The firemen couldn't put it out—'

'See?' Dad nodded at Larry. 'The Silver City is just burning away.'

But Tim couldn't be stopped now. 'Any minute the roof was going to go! There was a huge crowd—'

'Where are you going now, Bert?' Larry asked. Jean had dodged the question, Tim didn't want to hear it, but Larry had barged on in.

Jean and Tim looked at each other in sad understanding.

Dad looked at his black and seamed hands. 'I been thinking about it . . . maybe Queenstown. It's not so far away.'

Larry jerked his head in annoyance. 'Forget about the mines, Bert, they're dying. Come up river with me this time.'

Dad looked up at Larry as if he was floating in the air. 'The rivers?' Then he smiled and leaned back in his seat. 'Yeah. You seen the Thunderer yet?'

Larry scratched his beard. 'Not yet. Got no time.'

'Pity.' Dad winked at Tim.

Tim smiled back. For as long as he could remember Dad had talked about taking him 'Up The Rivers' to find the Thunderer—when he grew up enough. The Thunderer was Dad's name for a waterfall somewhere in the wild mountains, across Macquarie Harbour, up the Gordon River, the Franklin, past the Jane. A tremendous waterfall that nobody had ever seen.

'But you have heard it, haven't you, Larry?' said Tim.

'Oh, yes, I've heard it,' Larry said. 'It can't be reached because it's in the middle of a god-awful gorge. It sounds like some mountain is breaking apart and you can feel it through your boots.'

'You know, it's about time to try,' said Dad.

'Try what?'

'Reach the Thunderer. Now *that* would be worth the trip.'

'Come with me and we'll have a go. After we've got enough Huon pines to get you one of those funny new automobiles and to get Jean a mansion in Hobart. Okay?'

'I don't want a mansion in Hobart,' Jean said. 'I want—' she glanced at Tim. 'We just want a little more of Albert.'

Dad had not heard. 'Maybe we can take Tim with us.

26

He's pretty keen on the Huon pine, he should see where it comes from.'

Tim splashed in sudden excitement. 'Yeah!'

'Yeah, sure,' Larry shrugged.

'Why not?' Dad turned to Tim. 'We may not discover the Thunderer but we're going to see rivers, mountains, forests almost nobody knows about. We're going to have all the camping trips we never had rolled into one. Better than the wreck. I'll teach you how to cast for trout, maybe even pan for gold—'

'Now—'

Then Dad saw Jean's face. 'What d'you say, love?'

'Whatever you think,' Jean said, with no expression at all on her face.

'Yes—' Dad said slowly. 'When d'you want to go, Larry?'

'When it gets a bit warmer. A month, maybe.'

'Then that's it. I go to Queenstown for a month. If I get a job for a short time, that's fine. Pay for things at home and food on the rivers. If I can't get a job at Queenstown, well, Tim and I *have* to go on the rivers. Okay?'

Jean nodded, but she wasn't looking at Dad's face.

Tim took his Huon block to bed. He went to sleep listening for the Thunderer.

# 3

# A Little Revenge

Next morning Tim walked with Dad to the beginning of the overland track to Queenstown. He insisted on carrying Dad's swag—a blanket, a change of clothes, and some food—to show he wasn't all *that* little. He was big enough to find the Thunderer.

'It's going to be great, isn't it, Dad?' he panted. 'All those rough rivers and the forests to explore. Wait 'til I tell the kids.'

'Ah, I wouldn't tell them yet,' Dad said.

'Aren't we going, now?'

'Look son, you want to go, I want to go—I've been wanting to go for ten years. We are going. It's just that we don't leave for a month and a lot of things can happen in a month. So don't tell everyone, all right?'

'Yeah, sure.'

'You can stop now.'

'I can walk all the way to Queenstown with the swag,' panted Tim, brightly. But he was glad when the swag was lifted from his back.

'You just get ready. No fights with giants, no taking risks at all.' Dad squeezed Tim's shoulder. 'Remember, in four weeks we're after the Thunderer.'

Tim stood in the middle of the muddy track, watching Dad shoulder the swag and stride toward a pale yellow hill. He stopped for a moment, a small black shape on a distant crest, turned, waved and bobbed out of sight.

'Four weeks,' said Tim, and went home.

* * *

In the first week Larry took over as if he had ruled the house for years. But Jean quietly tolerated him, and when he sat down in the house baby Ian treated him like a mountain to be climbed. And Tim just sat in the sun and studied his Huon block.

A few years ago Tim had found a broken and rusty knife near an abandoned mine. The handle was of chipped, rotting wood and the ragged blade was no longer than his little finger, but Tim felt the knife had all the power of a wizard's wand. It changed things.

He worked on the blade for a month, until it flickered flawlessly as it shaved hardwood as if it were a carrot. He replaced the handle with one he carved of myrtle, then whittled branches down to twigs, blocks of timber to lopsided ships, until the blade seemed to be part of his hand. He stopped worrying about being the town 'shrimp'—what did it matter if he couldn't kick a ball thirty yards, couldn't make any school team, couldn't win a wrestle with almost anyone, if he could carve a dreadnought with lifeboats and revolving guns?

So Tim spent the first week studying the Huon block, looking for the secret shape he had found in every piece of wood. The shape might be a horse, a ship, a bird, a pirate's head; and when he saw it, all he had to do was cut the waste wood away and there it was. But this time it was hiding from him.

Dad sent a letter. He had moved into a camp with six other men in an old shack in Linda, high above Queenstown. He might get a temporary job at the 1000-foot level of the North Lyell mine after a miner there broke his arm. 'Bad luck for Ted,' Dad had written, 'but very good luck for us. Ted should be back in a month, and when he returns I leave. Sorry, Jean, but it looks like we find the Thunderer before I stay at home.'

★ ★ ★

In the second week Tim found the secret shape, but only after he met Coutts.

Tim was hauling an empty cart out to the bush to carry the wood Larry was about to cut for the house.

Coutts was carrying a length of pipe from a derelict house on the edge of town when he saw Tim. He stuck the pipe into the mud, leant on it and beamed. "'Allo, little Tim! What 'ave we 'ere?"

Tim stopped, and for a moment he was about to run. Instead he started to think very fast. 'A cart.'

'A cart for me? You shouldn't have.'

'For you?' And suddenly Tim smiled. 'You guessed. Hop in.'

Coutts frowned but he sprawled in the cart, prodding Tim with the pipe. 'Don't think you're going to dump me in the mud or you'll lose an ear.'

'Oh no, no, nothing like that.' Tim began to pull hard, back the way he'd come.

Coutts relaxed, idly urging Tim with the pipe. 'Thought you might be hiding from me. Whatcha been doing?'

'Digging a hole.' Tim panted.

'A hole?'

'In the bush. Very deep, the hole.'

'What d'you want with a great hole in the bush?'

'You can hide things for a long time in a hole.'

'What things?'

'Just . . . things.' Tim stopped and waved. 'Here he is, Larry. I got him!'

Coutts looked up the street and saw a huge man striding through the mud with a great axe on his shoulder, its blade flashing in the sun. Coutts thought for a moment of the cart he was sitting in, the mysterious hole deep in the bush and the giant with the axe. He leapt from the cart, dropped the pipe and bolted for the centre of Zeehan.

Larry scratched the side of his head with the blade of the axe. 'You aren't going to tell me what happened, are you?'

Tim, doubled over in laughter and clinging to the cart for support, only shook his head.

That night Tim began to carve a Maori mask from the Huon block, a fearsome mask with rolling, mean eyes and a huge tongue thrust from the side of the curling mouth.

Dad wrote to Jean: 'Well, love, I'm down the Mount Lyell shaft now and the money's rolling in. After the spell up the rivers we might be able to afford a holiday in Hobart. What do you think? You probably heard about the young bloke getting killed by a rock fall here, but don't worry about it. His brother keeps on running round and saying the mine's not safe, the roof'll fall in, there's only one way in or out . . . . We even went on a strike, but most of it was rubbish. See you soon.'

* * *

In the third week Tim's mask was beginning to look real enough to frighten Ian. Tim was very happy about this and decided that when it was finished he would hang it on his bedroom door.

Meanwhile he continued to help Larry get in the wood supply. After a long day with spelling and mental sums at the Big School, Tim would follow Larry into the bush, watching him drive the broad axe into the heavy wood.

'What's it like out there?' Tim asked after Larry brought down a tall dead tree so it fell exactly between two saplings without harming either of them.

Larry measured the trunk absently with the axe handle. 'Out where?'

31

'Out there in the forest. Is it dangerous?'

Larry lopped a branch off the trunk. 'Nah. Not if you're careful. 'Course there are still a few tigers about. And cannibals.' He swung one-handed at another dead branch.

Tim laughed.

Larry looked up seriously. 'What's funny?'

'Tigers and cannibals.'

'Oh yes. Didn't you know?' And he went on chopping.

Tim dismissed Larry's ridiculous claims with a shrug. 'Maybe I can work in the forest when I leave school.'

Larry hauled his axe from a log and looked at Tim. 'No,' he said. 'You can see it all when you're with your Dad, but that's it. You can't work on the rivers.'

'Why not?'

'You're too small.'

But because of the glorious victory over Coutts and his creation of the terrible Maori mask Tim had forgotten what 'small' meant.

'I'm twelve now,' he said.

Larry hefted the axe and threw it easily to Tim. 'Catch that.'

Tim raised his arms in fright, got his hands on the haft below the gleaming head and staggered back, and fell. He wasn't ready for the immense weight of the tool Larry carried like a twig. He lay on the ground with the axe-head on his stomach and he was having trouble just lifting it from his chest.

Larry bent forward and swept the axe away. 'Not too young. Too small,' he said.

★　★　★

On Saturday, the end of the fourth week, the Walker house was seething with excitement. Tomorrow Albert Walker would come home from Queenstown. He would rest for the day, then set off with Larry and Tim on Monday for Strahan, the rivers and the Thunderer.

'All right, just be damn careful.' Jean slammed a plate of burgoo—porridge—on the table in front of Tim. 'You hear?' She put her hands on her hips and glared at Larry.

Larry smeared some cocky's joy—golden syrup—over a couple of johnny cakes and nodded. 'We are very careful up there, Jean,' he said. 'We have to be.' He buried his nose in the long grey columns of the *Zeehan and Dundas Herald*. It was Saturday, October 12th, 1912.

'Shoog!' said Ian happily and banged his spoon on his wooden highchair.

'That goes for you—especially.' Jean prodded Tim hard with her finger. 'I'm letting you go against my better judgement.'

'I'll watch everything, really—'

'Gum!' Ian said and began to spoon sugar carefully into his mouth without disturbing the burgoo.

Larry slapped his paper. 'He'll be right. Tell you what, we'll celebrate tonight. Take in the Theatre Royal. All of us. My shout.'

'Oh Larry, it's very nice but we can't,' said Jean.

'Aw, Mum—'

'Rubbish. 'Course we can. They've got films on. *Pathe's Australian Gazette, A Sailor and His Lass.* You'll love it.'

'I don't know if that's the sort of film Tim should see.'

Tim agreed. But any film is better than no film at all.

'Ah, Tim can keep his eyes closed. There's a film for him—*Sheriff Jim's Last Shot.*'

'Yeah!' Tim fired a finger at Larry. 'Can we, Jean, can we?'

Jean smiled and nodded. 'Boys,' she sighed.

So Larry, Jean and Tim were walking down the main road of Zeehan in the early evening, in their best clothes, scrubbed and with the taste of a very good piece of steak still on their lips. Tim was thinking of what he'd like to do when he left school: if he couldn't become a sodden

33

piner like Larry, or a miner like Dad, he'd be a western lawman like Sheriff Jim, with one last shot in the dusty street of Abilene. Now there it would actually pay to be small; you'd be harder to hit.

Jean stopped outside Newman's dress shop and admired a grey tweed costume until Tim almost had to drag her after Larry. Larry had drifted into a quiet crowd outside the offices of the *Zeehan and Dundas Herald*, where a man wearing a black vizor was sticking some paper on the window from inside.

'What's up?' Larry said to a man who was closer to the window.

The man shrugged, and turned from the window. 'A little fire,' he said.

'Where?'

'Ah, North Lyell.' The man walked away.

The disaster had started.

# 4

# Disaster

Jean took in a sharp breath behind Larry as he barged into the crowd. Tim watched him shuffling forward, squinting, craning his neck until he was nodding at something, then he was shouldering his way back towards Jean.

'There's a fire at the pump house on the 700-foot level,' Larry said. 'Nowhere near Bert at the 1000-foot level. It should burn itself out soon enough, but the smoke is keeping some miners stuck down there. That's about it.'

'When did the fire start?'

'This morning.'

'This morning? And they're telling us now.'

'They didn't think it was serious. They don't think it's serious now.'

Jean pressed her lips together for a moment. 'What do you think, Larry?'

'I think they're right.'

'I should be there.'

'No point. It won't last and Bert's probably not down there anyway.'

Jean hesitated then nodded. 'Let's go home.'

'What about Sheriff Jim?' Tim said in sudden alarm. He could still see the happy crowd outside the Theatre Royal.

Jean looked at Tim as if she couldn't hear him, then past him as she walked stiffly towards home.

35

* * *

The next day, Sunday, Tim was sent to the newspaper office at the first glimmer of dawn to bring back any news. As he ran down the streets he thought: Larry will be right. He's always right. It will be all over by now. The cages will have whizzed all the miners up to the surface through any smoke, the fire will be out by now—there's not much to burn in a mine, is there? And Dad is now getting ready to come home. Probably on his way. We could have seen Sheriff Jim after all . . . .

There were a few cold people blowing steam at the *Herald's* window, but Tim could see the news slips easily. During the night one of the men's two cages had jammed at the 600-foot level while trying to push smoke out of the shaft. More than 200 miners had walked from another mine to help rescue their mates and had begun work on a narrow blocked shaft, the engine winze, which runs parallel to the main shaft from the 300-foot level. At the last count seventy miners had escaped from the burning mine, but ninety-six men were still trapped.

All this news had been stuck on the window before 1 am, but while Tim was reading the man working in the office slapped the latest from North Lyell before his nose.

At 6.45 am it said: 'Nothing new.'

No news for almost six hours.

Tim forgot about Sheriff Jim and ran home with something cold clutching at his throat.

* * *

Breakfast was very strained, with Jean talking in sudden bursts of short sentences followed by long silences. A neighbour came round and offered to look after Ian when Jean left for the mine.

'Thank you very much, Mrs Simmonds,' Jean said,

'but I'm waiting for a message from Albert. He's probably not down there at all.'

But when Mrs Simmonds left, Jean covered her eyes for a moment. 'Why can't they bring the miners up fast in the other cage? A little smoke never hurts anyone. Does it?'

★ ★ ★

In the afternoon Tim learned how deadly the smoke in the North Lyell had become. He saw a single rail motor—a bus adapted to run on a railway line instead of a road—barrelling into Zeehan station from Burnie, and ran after it. The station-master stopped ushering a few passengers into the rail motor long enough to shoo Tim away. After a few minutes the rail motor coughed and rattled toward Queenstown.

'Who were they, Mr Fahey?' Tim said when the rush was over.

'Mostly doctors, Tim.' The station-master sounded tired. 'And the brother of one of the miners. Only people needed at the mine. Oh, and two diving suits from Devonport.'

'A diving suit? Is the mine flooded as well?'

The station-master shook his head. 'No. It's to go through the smoke.'

'Only smoke? Why does a diver want to do that?'

'To find the miners.'

'Are they lost?'

The station-master started to say something, then checked himself. 'Ah, you're old enough. We don't know, but it's bad down there. They've found the body of a miner—not Albert—close to the top.'

Tim had to cough to talk. 'Mum says a little smoke never hurt anyone.'

'It's what in it that counts. The fire has changed the air in the mine into carbon monoxide gas. You breathe that for a few minutes and you go to sleep. A few minutes more and you die. That's why we need diving suits. They're not good, but they're all we've got.'

'Oh,' said Tim. In a handful of hours the thrill of the river trip had curdled into a nightmare and there was nothing he could do about it.

* * *

He's down there,' Jean said quietly that night. She looked old, white and very tired.

Tim hunched in his chair, squeezed Dad's block of wood and became a rock. Nothing hurts rocks and rocks never hear anything.

'You seen a list?' Larry's voice was strangely gentle.

'It's not in order but he's there all right. Half-way down the second column. Albert Walker. I knew he was down there from the first night, when he didn't let me know he was all right. I should have gone up there first thing. Walked the Overland.'

'There's a train tomorrow morning.'

'Yes. Are you coming?'

'No, love. I'm helping out on the railways. They're going to need equipment quick. I can do more here to speed things up.'

'Look after Tim?'

'Sure.'

I am a bloody rock, thought Tim. But he felt himself crumbling.

* * *

On Monday morning Jean carried a wailing Ian next door and planted him firmly in the arms of Mrs Simmonds. Then she kissed and squeezed Tim for a long time, kissed Larry damply on the cheek and stepped aboard a crowded

38

train. A few hours before some smoke helmets from Launceston had been railed through.

Larry stepped up to the side of the carriage and winked. 'Buck up. He's been in worse spots before. Once he was almost run down by a runaway train. My nipper can take care of himself.'

After the train had left, Larry and Tim walked from the station to the *Herald* office. They learned that a diver called Chambers had tried to put out the fire at the 700-foot pump house and failed. He had also tried to find any miners and failed again. An attempt had been made to free the stuck cage and had failed so badly that both cages in the mine were now stuck. The fire was raging uncontrolled in the mine and the trapped miners could not escape.

But there were some glimmers of hope.

'We're getting decent help at last, Tim.' Larry flicked his nail on the window. 'Hobart is sending us their top fireman, Trousselot, in his own train. Started at midnight. And Melbourne is now sending a shipful of smoke jackets and helmets and experts on the *Lady Loch*. We can do it.'

\* \* \*

In the afternoon a long rope was lowered into the mine with a lamp, a board and a pencil attached. It snaked through the heavy smoke, past the jammed cage 600 feet from the surface, past the still glowing fire round the blackened pump at 700 feet, then down past silent tunnels in the rock until it stopped at 1000 feet, the bottom of the mine. The lamp moved the deep shadows on the walls as it swayed slowly in invitation.

It was not touched.

\* \* \*

Tim did not go to school that day. When Larry left him to help clear the railway he wandered to the cemetery with his Maori mask, sat under a tree and waited for trains. Under his slow knife the mask seemed to be laughing at him.

He was about to go home to cook something for Larry when the train from Hobart arrived. Tim could place it half a mile away; the locomotive was a stranger to the West Coast and it was only pulling one carriage. It had taken seventeen hours to travel from Hobart to Zeehan but that wasn't bad at all. To reach Zeehan the train had to cross Tasmania from south to north, then almost from east to west and finally south from Burnie, covering three quarters of a circle.

The train stopped at the station and men hurriedly began to disconnect the locomotive from the carriage as a very tall man in a black uniform leapt down from it and strode towards the centre of town.

Tim was trying to work out what the fireman, Trousselot—it had to be Trousselot—was doing in Zeehan when he saw Coutts coming towards him.

He didn't want Coutts any time, but now was too much. He jammed his legs under him but resisted the temptation to run.

Coutts looked up and stopped as if he had just seen Tim. But then he kept on coming. 'Walker—' he said, and petered out.

Tim waited.

'About your dad—' he shrugged. 'I'm sorry.' He turned and walked away.

Tim stared in astonishment at Coutts' retreating back. 'Ah . . . thanks.'

Coutts stopped and looked back. 'Yeah. Well—'

There was something else. 'Is there any news?'

Coutts came back slowly, reluctantly. 'How long you been here?'

'Hours.'

Coutts looked relieved. 'There's a fast ship coming from Melbourne.'

'I know. The *Lady Loch*. Been coming since early this morning.'

'Yeah, well you don't know this one. It's the *Loongana*. They call it the 'Greyhound of the Sea', it's so fast. It's got smart blokes from the mines at Ballarat and Bendigo and the new Draeger smoke helmets. It left Melbourne an hour ago. And there's a train with the steam up waiting in Burnie for them.'

'Oh. Tremendous.' But there was something else. 'And?'

Coutts scuffed his boots in the mud. 'Just what they're saying.'

'Yeah?'

'Look, they're just saying it, they don't know. Just because they found a coupla bodies they say there's nobody alive in the mine.'

\* \* \*

Tim almost ran into the tall fireman leading a procession of men carrying thick pipe on their shoulders. He skipped aside and stopped.

He thought, bleakly: so he's got something like a diver's suit and that lot will put him further down the mine. So what? What's the good of locos from Hobart, helmets from Launceston, ships from Melbourne, trains from Burnie, if there's nobody left to rescue?

Tim wandered home and put some soup on without caring much what he was doing.

But Larry burst into the house like a circus parade, hands wide, mouth open, laughing and shouting: 'D'y'ear? Did you hear? Eh?'

Larry sighed, a balloon going down. 'Ah, kid, kid. They've got a message to us. The miners on 1000-foot

41

level. Like: "Forty men in 40 stope. Send food and candles at once. No time to lose." All we have to do is reach them!'

At that moment Tim decided that he must be on that rescue train from Burnie. No matter what.

# 5

# Number Three

Tim rolled out of bed at five o'clock next morning, feeling
that somehow there was something different in the air.
The old smells were still there, damp wood, smoke and a
touch of sulphur from the distant smelter, and there were
the old sounds, the dripping of water from the roof, the
steady beat of a steam engine in a dying mine, and
the quacking of ducks across the street. But there was
something . . . .

Tim hauled his black guernsey over his head, and
stopped.

Of course.

He popped his head clear of the heavy wool.

This was the day he was going to rescue Dad. On a
train.

Tim dressed quietly so he could sneak out of the house
before Larry woke up and stopped him. But he knocked
his carved block to the hard wood floor.

'Stupid!' he hissed, scooped the block up from between his feet and waited for Larry to stride into his
room.

There was no sound at all from Larry, so Tim crept
towards the back door carrying the block as if it were a
gold egg. He reached for the doorknob when he saw the
note on the kitchen table.

It said:

Gone to help fettlers keep line
cleer for train. Eat and go to
schoole. Home tonite.
Larry


Tim relaxed and smirked a little over Larry's spelling.
He realized he was carrying the block and put it on the
table. He poured cocky's joy over some bread, tried to
get his lips around the syrup without smearing it all over
himself, and the ugly face on the block rolled its wooden
tongue at him in disgust. He stopped eating half-way
through a bite.

He didn't know where his train was.

The train that was waiting at Burnie last night with its
fire glowing for the *Lady Loch* and the *Loongana* might be
thundering toward Zeehan, loaded with smoke helmets
and experts from Victoria. It may be in Zeehan station
now!

Tim stood up to ram a chunk of bread, his knife and—
after a moment's hesitation—the block into a hessian bag.
He ran from the house, trailing long glistening threads of
syrup from his chin.

He was alarmed when he saw a strange locomotive at
the station, but this one did not seem to be in a hurry.
The fireman lounged in the cabin and casually fed the fire
with just enough coal to keep engine hissing steam. The
carriages behind the polished green and black loco were
empty.

''As the train gone, sir?' Tim shouted.

The fireman, a short, dark man with flushed cheeks,
straightened, looked at Tim's syrup whiskers and smiled.
'The *Burnie Flyer*? Today, she's a flyer.'

Tim nodded urgently.

'You're not missin' her yet. Take a while.'

Tim smiled in relief.

The fireman squatted on the footplate. 'Why d'you
want to know?'

Tim dodged the question. 'M'dad's down the mine.'

'Ah.' The fireman wiped his hands on the knees of his blue dungarees and jumped down from the loco. 'I'm Paddy Hartnett. What's your name, lad?'

Tim told him.

'Don't remember Walker on the list. There are so many of them. Don't you worry. You hear what happened this mornin', then?'

Tim started to shake his head; then he saw the Hobart loco on a nearby track, quiet and still. 'The big fireman? Did he save them?'

'Trousselot? Ah, no. He tried but he was too big a man. Found that the smoke helmets were only good for twenty minutes, no good at all. He wore somethin' like a suit of armour and got down to the pump house, but he couldn't squeeze any further. The miners are still down there—now it's up to us to get them out. Eh?'

Tim looked up at Paddy and made some calculations. He had planned to creep on board the train when nobody was looking, but maybe, just maybe, this fireman would allow him on the train if he just asked.

'No, I didn't mean Trousselot,' Paddy said. 'I meant the ships. Bass Strait hit the *Lady Loch* with a howlin' storm, openin' up her decks—'

'She's sunk, then?' Tim hissed. For a moment he could see the wreck he and Dad had found near Trial Harbour, a metal-hulled old schooner with the waves seething through her broken back and the shattered masts trembling in the foam. Then it was exciting, now horrifying.

'No, no.' Paddy shook his head. 'The *Lady* almost had to give up the race, but she didn't. She made the Burnie breakwater before dawn and the flyer whistled her in.

'Then the captain of the *Lady* looked back at the storm— and saw the *Loongana*, lit up like a thousan' Christmas trees flyin' out of the black water.'

Tim stared at Paddy and suddenly grinned. It had

already changed. Today was going to be different. Nothing could go wrong.

'That's more like it, lad. The *Loongana* left Melbourne twelve hours behind the *Lady Loch* and caught the *Lady* in thirteen hours forty-five minutes. They won't break that record for a long, long time. Now it's up to us to keep up the pace.'

'Then you'll be taking the Melbourne men on to Strahan?'

'We won't just be going to Strahan, lad. We'll be going all the way. See our plates?' Paddy pointed to the polished brass plates on the sides of the locomotive's rich green cabin.

Tim read the plates. '*Mount Lyell Number Three*.' That was easy. Big letters, no higher than he was. But above, in smaller writing in a diamond: 'Dubs and Company, Glasgow Locomotive Works. 1898. It's come a long way.'

'Keep on reading.'

'What?' Tim frowned and then found the third plate. 'Oh. Abt system. Abt system?'

'It means she's a mountain loco, with a lovely heart for climbin'.' Paddy squatted by the loco's wheels and beckoned Tim beside him. 'Look there.'

There were the usual four big wheels and two smaller wheels, all connected to each other and to the black steam chest behind the buffers by the piston rods. Tim knew all this. But there was another wheel Tim had never seen before, an ugly, black cog wheel suspended under the loco's belly that touched nothing and seemed to be utterly useless.

'That's your Abt, Tim,' Paddy said. 'With it—and the sand boxes—we can gnaw our way up a mountain. It's a wonderful sight to see.'

Tim sucked in a short breath and talked very fast. 'Can I come in the train then? I'm small, I'm light, you wouldn't know I was there, I've got to be at the mine—'

46

He ran out of breath and Paddy was waving him into silence.

Paddy frowned and looked hard at Tim's bag. 'I don't know, lad. What about your mother?'

'She's up the mine.'

Paddy sucked a tooth and shrugged. Finally he said, 'We'll have to see. What are you like at polishin' engines?'

Tim spent three hours and fourteen minutes crawling over *Mount Lyell Number Three*, polishing the brass rim of the tall smokestack, wiping the glass of the large light before the smokestack, rubbing the grime from between the large green regulator dome and the whistle, cleaning the copper steam pipes until they shimmered, even rubbing the buffers clear of ore dust. But he kept an eye on the growing crowd of spectators in the station and on the empty railroad north.

Then someone shouted in excitement: 'There she is!'

At first it was no more than a puff of smoke above the forest but people began craning, leaning over the rails. The smoke grew to a small black circle floating above the shining rails, whistling urgently as it swept towards the station. The crowd on the station whistled back, throwing hats in the air and cheering.

The driver of *Mount Lyell Number Three* hurried across the rails and was pulled up into the engine by Paddy. Like Paddy, he was wearing blue dungarees and a cap, but he was older, with his hair flecked with grey, leaner and taller. He looked as stern as the headmaster at the Big School, and that troubled Tim. Perhaps he should have sneaked aboard the carriage after all.

'Fast enough for you, Peter?' asked Paddy, shovelling coal.

'They cut the time by three hours,' said Peter Jack in a rumbling Scottish burr. 'We'll be stretching ourselves to do as well.'

'Shut yer eyes and we'll damn well fly.'

'Shut yer eyes and you'll swim in the Henty. Who's the lad?'

Tim was standing by the footplate, looking up at Peter with a dirty rag in his hands.

'Tim. Got a father in the mine.' Paddy wasn't looking at Tim at all.

'Mother?'

'Up there.'

'Put him in the carriage then.'

'Ah, he's only a matchbox of a kid.'

Peter looked down at Tim and then at the slowing train, settling in a cloud of rising steam. The train had arrived at Zeehan at 10.30 am, four hours and twenty-six minutes after it had left Burnie. The normal run took more than seven hours. But now the excitement had died and grim-faced men jumped from the still-moving train and carried large boxes to *Number Three*. They were followed by a confused group of men and women; three of the women had been crying. One woman of about sixty-five stopped between the two trains, looked at Tim and stumbled into the *Mount Lyell*'s carriage with her head bowed and her shoulders shaking.

Peter looked at Tim as if he were sizing him up like a bag of potatoes, and for the first time in his life Tim wished he was a little smaller. But Peter sighed and beckoned. 'Come up here, boy. Quickly!'

Tim stepped toward the engine with a furtive grin dancing round his face, to be yanked into space and bounced into a semicircular niche, high in the rear wall of the cabin. He fitted into the niche as though the loco was built around him. He could see in front and behind through large round windows, he could rest his right hand on the tall column of the hand brake and he could see every flicker, every move, in the awesome battery of gauges, levers and wheels that drove the loco.

Tim's eyes glistened. Peter Jack and Paddy Hartnett might seem to be doing the work here, but *he* was the captain, the chief engineer. Dad would be out of the mine and safe in a couple of winks. It couldn't go any other way.

'Boy, you keep a good grip and stay out of the way,' said Peter, with a warning nod. 'I don't even want to know that you're here.'

'Yessir,' said Tim.

Peter looked back at the guard's van as Paddy cranked the hand brake off, pushing Tim's legs to one side. The green flag flashed from the rear of the train.

Peter pulled the lever, and the brass whistle on the regulator dome shrieked. Paddy rammed his short shovel into the small opening below Tim's feet, and threw coal at the closed iron gates by Peter's legs. The gates slammed open, allowed the coal to reach the fire and slammed shut again.

Peter moved a long black lever before him, the adhesive throttle. Steam scorched up from the boiler to the regulator dome, the green hump before the cabin, down heavy copper pipes to the steam chests before the wheels and pushed hard against the piston rods. The rods thrust against the wheels until they spun a little and the locomotive hissed, clanked and began to move.

Eight minutes after the Emu Bay train had finished her dash of eighty-eight twisting miles from Burnie to Zeehan, *Mount Lyell Number Three* was rolling towards Strahan.

# 6

# The Train Dash

In the beginning everything was moving very slowly. Peter adjusted a wheel as if he was cleaning it, Paddy pushed a lazy shovel of coal at the fire gates and the carriages lurched reluctantly on the rails. Tim watched the steam misting round the hump of the regulator dome, the great balls of black smoke lifting tiredly from the tall smokestack, and he wanted to leap from the loco and push.

Then a cloud of smoke and steam swept over the train, covering Tim in a warm, brown fog. He heard the rhythm of the wheels change from a heavy mine pump to the canter of Steve Dodd's horses, to a roll of kettle drums. Now he felt the wind, saw Paddy hurl coal as Peter jerked a long lever to open the gates—so simple—and the smoke was curling high behind them.

Zeehan had vanished. The red roofs had faded into rolling hills of yellow button grass, the high clumps by the track spreading out into sweeping waves of gold on the crests. He had jumped from clump to clump many times on those hills, always scratching himself on the brittle grass spears, and always having to clutch at the dark seed boxes—the 'buttons'—for balance; but now he was almost flying over them.

'Okay,' said Paddy, and stood up. He had stopped shovelling, but the loco continued to accelerate.

By the time the train reached the smelters the wind was

pulling hard at Tim's hair and he wanted to shout, just for the hell of it. He expected a cheer as the train thundered between the tall chimneys of the smelters and the manager's house, but nothing happened. Men just stood by the nana carts and watched the train, their long-handled shovels forgotten by their sides.

'Hey!' Tim waved at them.

Nobody moved. As if they couldn't see him at all. But Peter turned and looked at him with a face like stone. Tim's arm froze in the air and withered.

'Don't they know we're the rescuers?' Tim said softly.

Paddy half-smiled. 'We haven't rescued anyone yet, kid. They'll cheer enough when we come back.'

The train raced down a shallow valley beside a creek dyed crimson by button grass roots. A shed pretending to be a station flickered past, a wooden bridge strode across a small river. Tim forgot about the men at the smelter. The rails under the loco were moving, rocking and jerking on their sleepers as the locomotive hit them.

'Is it safe?' Tim yelled into the wind.

'No!' Paddy shouted. And grinned.

A ragged crowd of thin sassafras trees jostled down a hill, their mottled trunks and thick foliage blocking out the sun. A moment later they were gone, the button grass sweeping toward a new hill. Tim had never travelled as fast as this before in his life.

'Long way to go,' said Paddy. 'But we're doing all right. Any other time we have to keep our speed down so we can watch out for trouble. This time we trust the fettlers to keep our track clear.'

A rock wall rose out of the grass and rushed toward the loco. Tim opened his mouth and started to shout something when the grassy hills vanished. The train was now skidding along a cliff with the roar of the loco booming back from the rock. To his left he could almost touch the sheer wall rearing far above the loco's smokestack, a wall alive with an avalanche of white flowers and light green moss. To his right there was nothing.

Nothing, until he looked down. At his foot the long, thin leaves of gum trees clattered about the fuzzy, many-beaked monsters of the banksia seed pods, but the great columns of their trunks were far below him. He glimpsed the dim caverns formed by the trees on the dark forest floor and realized that if the train jumped its tracks at this speed it would have a long way to topple.

A few seconds later they were racing down gentle hills to sand dunes and the sea. Tim relaxed a little.

He turned and looked into the first carriage. Miners were sitting calmly on their mysterious boxes, looking out the windows and rubbing knees with strangely-pale people from the East. One man, a very dignified gentleman in a tweed suit, cellulose collar, bow tie and handlebar moustache, was attempting to write in a jerking notebook.

He's a mainland newspaper reporter, thought Tim. We're going to make history!

Tim smiled. Of course! Today those ships crossed Bass Strait like it was a puddle, the Burnie train made a record they'll never break and we can't be stopped. Today isn't going to be great, today *is* great!

Peter pulled the throttle back and the loco's rush began to die.

Ahead a sand dune was held back from the track by tethered branches, but some of the sand had slid down the slope to the rail and a few men were shovelling with their backs to the speeding train.

Peter glanced at Paddy with a slight frown. He pulled the whistle, a short shriek of anger.

The fettlers kept on shovelling.

Tim frowned. What was wrong with them, couldn't they hear?

'Clowning about,' grunted Peter and reached for the whistle lever again.

The fettlers looked up at the train and began to stroll

52

from the line when it was no more than a hundred yards away and shaking the rails.

The last fettler, a big man, stepped from the line with an easy stride just clear of the shrieking loco.

'Move yer pins!' Peter yelled at him.

And the big fettler smiled a little, cocked his head—and saw Tim.

It was Larry. For a moment the man and the boy stared at each other, the smile fading on Larry's face as he shrank rapidly into the distance. In a few seconds it was not Larry any more, just a black figure standing on the pale sand of the dune with other black figures.

Then the figure hefted his long shovel and speared the sand six feet away.

Tim knew he would be in trouble. Tomorrow.

But today Tim could leave Larry and his anger round a bend of the track and concentrate on the rescue.

Suddenly the rolling dunes were swept aside by a clatter and a blur. Hard girders framed a broad river drifting through a still, green forest. Then it was gone and there was nothing left of the bridge but the ringing in Tim's ears.

'Big Henty,' said Paddy. 'We're getting there.'

The train slipped past a marsh in the sand, crossed a broad creek and Paddy pounded Tim's arm.

'Strahan,' he said. 'That was the easy bit.'

The train passed scattered houses on the button grass, always with people out front and watching the train, then the massive grey buildings of Strahan. It blew steam like an exhausted runner, but kept rolling through the town, through the quiet waterfront, before stopping behind a rail motor by the yawning ore chutes of Regatta Point.

Peter stepped back from the controls and wiped his hands. 'Well, that's my lot.'

'The time, Peter?' Paddy was watching men with water hoses and coal hurrying to *Number Three* as the miners staggered with their cases of Draeger helmets to the rail

53

motor. The miners looked a little whiter now. Tim wondered if he should run after them.

Paddy looked up at the sky. 'The run is usually 100 minutes. We did it in sixty-five. Cut off thirty-five minutes. How's that, then?'

Peter shrugged. 'Not bad.' And he jumped off the loco.

Tim saw that the rail motor was moving down the line, without some of the men who had carried the helmets, but more important, without *him*. He grabbed his bag, jumped from the tender with a yelp—and landed in the arms of the heavy man below.

The man grunted and held up Tim like an undersized fish. 'Hokay, what is this?' The man was almost shouting in a voice that wanted to speak German. 'Do we throw it away—or keep it?'

'Keep it, Barney,' Paddy said. 'It polishes locos. Move us.'

Barney Westerman vaulted onto the cabin with Tim slung over his shoulder. He pulled the whistle and a dozen men jostled outside the carriage doors. Tim was flipped casually into his hard seat but he noticed with relief that the train was moving again. The rail motor had disappeared.

Paddy explained Tim in less than a minute and Barney, *Number Three*'s second driver, greeted Tim with a sympathetic nod as the loco picked up speed on the flat rim of the vast brown Macquarie Harbour.

'What is in the bag, boy?'

Tim opened the bag for Barney and Barney pulled the carved block from the bag with a frown. The Maori mask rolled its eyes and thrust its long tongue at him; it wore a sticky sandwich like a hat.

'A head?' said Barney. 'What you want with this?'

'I made it. It's a present for Dad.'

'Ah.' Barney put the mask back in the bag. 'A present is a good thought.'

'If it doesn't frighten him to death,' Paddy said.

54

The loco turned from the turbulence of the harbour into the narrow valley of King River. There were several large logs being herded like cattle toward a noisy steam launch by men in punts with long poles.

Paddy followed Tim's gaze. 'King Billy pine, sassafras, Huon pine for the sawmills at Piccaninny Point. Piners. They all got web feet.'

'My uncle's a piner.'

'Bet he quacks.' Paddy shovelled coal into the fire.

Tim wanted to tell Paddy that he and Dad were going to be piners too and they were going to find the greatest waterfall in the world . . . . Then he decided to let things lie.

King River was now black water, carrying a trace of green slime as it eddied between broad stretches of heavy yellow mud and blackened stumps. Manferns stood like patient spectators with umbrellas beside the track as the train slid into a dark green tunnel of trees and undergrowth.

Barney pointed ahead. 'End of level track, boy. Teepookhana.'

Tim had learnt about the river port at school, but this was the first time he had seen it. It was a disappointment. Teepookhana—Tasmanian Aboriginal for kingfisher— had been the third busiest port in Tasmania until the railway had taken the boats away. Now it was a little station and a few wooden houses beginning to rot on a gentle slope into the quiet, black river.

Barney reluctantly decelerated as the train drew an echo from the port and slid over the river on a tall iron bridge.

'Now we start to climb,' said Barney. He pushed the throttle home but the loco could not go any faster.

'Abt?' asked Tim.

Barney shook his head. 'Not yet.'

The train was climbing steeply, slowing down as the carriages became heavier. The forest pressed in, smothering the smoke as it left the stack. Something in the forest was roaring.

55

Now they were on another bridge, a bridge so long Tim could not see the other end. The bridge lifted from the forest on wooden trestles which changed to iron as it soared across the river.

'Quarter Mile Bridge,' Paddy shouted over the roar. 'Isn't she great?'

The bridge was being shaken by the roar. The loco reached the metal part of the bridge with a clang and a rumble, and the river was no longer a quietly-moving, black lake. It was shouldering its way out of a narrow gorge, battering at the bridge and hurling spray over the smokestack. *Number Three* looked small, a child's toy on a bridge of matchsticks.

Tim looked straight down at the seething water and for a moment he felt that the loco was toppling, plunging toward the river. Then he heard the slow pounding of the engine become a drum roll, and the train clattered from the bridge into the forest again. He was surprised to see that his left hand was trembling a little, but he ignored it.

The loco rocked and shuddered, swallowing the shining tracks almost as fast as in the dash to the sea. He thought he saw the rail motor ahead and started to look out for the first houses of Queenstown.

We're almost there, Dad, he thought. All of us. For a moment Tim could even hear words in the racketing rhythm of the wheels, we are coming for you, coming for you, coming . . .

Then the train stopped. Men rushed from a muddy station called Dubbil Barril and filled *Number Three* with water, as Barney tapped his watch.

'Now we use Abt,' said Paddy.

The line ahead became three rails, not two, as it clawed up a very long and steep hill. A hill you might get a fit donkey to climb, not a train.

'The rail in the middle is for the Abt system. The cogged wheel, remember?' said Paddy.

'Come on. We have no time to talk-talk. Give me some

steam please.' Barney blasted the whistle once and opened the left throttle.

Paddy glared at Barney, but he began to shovel. 'Everyone else starts the Abt wheel now, before we reach the rack line,' he grunted. 'So the wheel rolls smooth onto the rack.'

'Everyone else is anyone else,' said Barney.

There was a heavy crash beneath the loco, the grinding of heavy machinery as it was forced to move. Paddy moved the second long lever, the auxiliary throttle, and the grinding became a steady gnawing. Tim watched the third line—really two parallel teethed bars close to each other—sliding under the black snout of the loco. Then he was pushed back in his seat as the loco tilted and began to climb.

Tim looked back into the carriage and saw standing men lean as if they wanted to touch the floor without bending their knees. He thought that this must be what it is like to fly, then he looked at the trees beside the track and saw that the train was moving so slowly he could almost walk alongside it. No, it wasn't like flying. Sitting in this shuddering, clanking, panting machine slowly hauling itself up a mountain in rolling waves of steam was like nothing in the world.

The train climbed for three miles to the lonely station of Rinadeena, then plummeted for a mile and a half on an even steeper stretch of Abt to Halls Creek, with Barney plying the brakes and the outer wheels squealing.

But after that the line levelled and straightened. *Number Three* built up steam, flattening the smoke from her stack as she raced past the first barren hills of Queenstown.

Tim leant forward in his seat, eyes wide and triumphant as he listened to the wheels thundering down the track.

*Coming for you, coming, coming . . . .*

# 7

# The Mine

It didn't last. Tim watched the dark green forests fade quickly into country straight out of a 'Sheriff Jim' movie—stark hills of orange, yellow and white. There were no trees at all on these hills, not even a bush. Tim had heard that everything round Queenstown had been killed by axemen, floods and sulphur from the mine smelters, but he hadn't been ready for the desolation. A plume of dirty smoke was rising from a distant hill.

'What's that?' he asked Paddy.

'It's the mine.'

And *Number Three* stopped speaking to him.

The train roared between bald hills, beside a river so dirty it looked like flowing lava, through a goods shed, past the Queenstown station and on to the mine sheds. Barney stopped the train, yanked Tim from his seat, wound the emergency brake on, and sagged slightly, a very tired man.

'What is the time, Paddy?' He was watching his passengers step down unsteadily from the carriages.

'Twelve forty-two. We did it in an hour. Half the time for the normal run. They'll never do that again. *We'll* never do it again.'

'Just so it does some good.'

Paddy slapped the solid German on the shoulder and turned to Tim. 'We've finished. You haven't. A little more to go. Up there.'

'Up there' was the side of a muddy hill, so steep that clods of clay continuously rolled and bumped to the bottom. But a railway went straight up to the summit, like a metal ruler leaning on the hill to show how steep it was.

Tim picked up his bag and jumped from *Number Three*, running a few paces before he turned and waved at Paddy and Barney. He didn't even try to smile. Paddy raised a thumb and winked, but Tim was swept on by a panting rush of passengers from *Number Three*.

Ahead, men were sitting in adapted ore carts, but there was no engine. There was no point in having one, because it was impossible for any loco—including *Number Three*—to climb the hill. The reporter in the tweed suit was dusting a seat in the last cart as Tim climbed in beside him.

Almost immediately the carts jerked, clanged and moved forward and up. There was no sound beyond the nervous talk of the passengers and the squeaking of the wheels, but the carts rose smoothly above the rust-marked roofs of the mine sheds. Tim had to cling onto the edge of his cart to prevent himself from falling backwards down the slope.

The reporter saw the bewilderment on Tim's face. 'It's a haulage line, lad.'

'Oh, yes,' Tim said. 'Of course.'

Tim looked ahead at the line, now spreading wooden wings to keep the rolling clay from the rails. There was a long straight rope from the lead cart to the summit of the hill, taut and humming like a string on a fiddle.

'But what if the rope breaks?' Tim was looking down at the tiny men at the base of the line.

'We have a very quick return trip,' the reporter said.

Tim stared at the fragile rope until the carts stopped. He could see the very small engine that had hauled the carts up the slope, a No 7 Krauss engine called 'Sloshey', a few wooden huts and the mouth of the North Lyell mine.

There were more than a hundred people standing in groups around the square entrance, women in light grey dresses, or tweed with a little fur, head-hugging hats, men in dark suits or stained waistcoats. Everyone looked grim.

Tim saw some miners erecting what looked like a canvas funnel further down the hill at the smaller entrance to the engine winze, the shaft that ran parallel to the main shaft. Two miners from Victoria carried a box between them into the main entrance, their faces distorted by strange masks. Coal fires were blazing round the mine.

After twenty minutes of searching through the groups Tim found Jean, standing alone near a shed. She looked very lonely.

'Hello Mum,' he said quietly.

She looked at him for a while, as if trying to remember who he was, then she took two paces toward him and crushed him to her body.

'Oh God,' she said. 'What are you doing here? Where's Larry?'

'How's Dad?'

'I think he's all right, Tim. I really do. They've got fifty-one miners down there and they are going to get a full list up to us soon.'

'Nobody *knows* if Dad's there?'

'No. We have just to wait.'

Tim felt the roaring glory of the train dash die in his hands. After streaking past the button-grass hills, the sheer cliff, the bridge over the cauldron, the mountain climbing, after everything, there was still nothing he could do. He shared his bread with Jean and carved strange patterns in the cheeks of his Maori mask until half-past three in the afternoon, waiting for something to happen. He wondered what had happened to the men and the helmets from Victoria.

Then J. Ryan sent a list of the miners he had with him down the mine at 40 stope.

A haggard man in a dripping bowler hat started to read from a stained piece of paper and people round the tunnel mouth ran towards him. Tim squeezed past the furiously-scribbling reporter to hear;

'Lambert, T; Hayes, J; Walker, E; Lock—'

He rushed back to Jean and found her, still tense and listening to the man. She mustn't have heard the name. 'Mum! Dad's there! He's—'

'Shut up,' said Jean harshly, and kept on listening.

The man stopped reading and passed the paper to another man to display it. Jean looked like a rag doll, kept on her feet by a thread.

'He's there, Mum,' Tim tried again. 'I heard his name.'

'You heard E Walker, Tim. It wasn't Albert.'

'Oh,' Tim said very softly.

Jean reached out for him and squeezed his arm. 'I'm being silly, Tim. E or A, sounds the same; they've just made a mistake.'

'Yes. They've made a mistake. Dad's down there.'

'We've just got to wait.'

'He'll be up soon.'

The sun dipped and set. The men and women waiting on the muddy slope moved near to the coal fires, talked a little and sipped some soup.

Tim walked away from a fire in time to see two miners carrying the Draeger helmets from the tunnel. They were surrounded by other men, but Tim had seen one of the men in the carriage of *Number Three*.

'What did you find?' One of the men was asking.

The miner shrugged. 'We found some bodies on the way.'

'Many?'

'A few.'

'Okay, but did you get to see Ryan's blokes?'

'Yeah. In the end. God, it's a long way.'

'How were they?'

'You wouldn't believe it.'

'Why?'

'They were singing. Down there in that dripping rock for almost a hundred hours, and they were singing like they were in the pub.'

Tim ran back with the news to Jean, who seemed too tired to care.

Through the night men shouted at each other and plodded about with wire, rope and canvas. Tim tried to work out what they were doing, but Jean fell asleep and it was very hard to stay awake alone.

He was jerked from a muddy blanket against a wall by the roar of mighty machines almost shaking the mountain. He left Jean to walk down to the winze, now with some sort of gigantic elephant standing over it in the pale dawn.

As Tim approached the winze the elephant became a canvas funnel with two great fans pushing wind into it and down the winze. As Tim watched smoke from the bottom of the mine began to billow out of the main tunnel. The wind down the winze would stir the fire in the mine, but it might clear the air enough for the trapped miners to climb to freedom.

Tim returned to Jean at a run but he slithered to a stop when he saw Larry, holding his carved head. For a moment he thought of retreating to the winze, but Larry half turned and saw him.

'He's back,' Larry said, and Tim moved forward with a shrug.

But Larry had other things on his mind now. He nodded shortly at the boy and helped Jean to her feet.

'They're sending a wind into the mine,' Tim said helpfully.

'Good,' said Larry. 'That'll help. We'll know soon enough. What's this for?' He held up the head.

'It's for Dad—' For the first time Tim saw the anger in

the mask he had carved. Perhaps he should not give it to Dad when he came out of the mine. Not yet.

But Larry nodded and passed the head to Tim. 'Okay. Hang onto it.'

A little later a woman with a funny little hat pinned to her hair stopped by them. 'They say the miners are coming up now,' she said.

Jean stiffened, put her arm on Tim's shoulder and followed Larry to the dark, silent crowd around the entrance to the main tunnel.

'Dad's all right,' Tim said. 'You'll see.'

The morning warmed to a clear sun. The hundreds of relatives and miners who had spent their nights waiting by the tunnel were joined by more than a thousand people plodding up the hill from Queenstown or along the ridge from Linda, just to see the trapped miners walk free.

Far below, the miners were beginning to be brought along the 40 stope to the 1000-foot level, past the blocked shaft where they had sent their desperate messages to the surface by rope. They reached the bottom of the winze, now sighing with forced wind, and climbed 160 feet of narrow, slippery ladder. They were lifted by cage to the 700-foot level, where the fire was still burning, then they climbed 300 feet through passes and sets of timber. One by one, they were strapped into a bucket and hauled to the main tunnel.

'I can see their candles!' Tim shouted and pointed at the moving glow deep in the tunnel.

'Mrs Walker?' A grave-faced young man with a tie and a clean face leaned toward her.

A heavy miner stepped into the tunnel entrance. 'Can you hear me?' he bellowed. 'The first miners are comin' now. But they're fearsome tired, so no cheers, all right?'

'Yes?' Jean said to the young man.

'I'm afraid your husband is not on the list. It's somebody else.'

Jean nodded and turned away.

63

Two miners stepped from the tunnel, drenched, blinded by the sun and supported by other miners. They were greeted by a guilty and ragged cheer as they moved down to the haulage line.

'Oh, God.' Jean suddenly swept her hand to her head. 'Why did I let him go—'

Larry squeezed her shoulder. 'Hey. That wasn't your fault. He wanted a little money before the rivers. Now come on.'

Tim stood beside Jean and Larry for a long afternoon, filled with other people's sudden happiness and their own endless silence. In the beginning Tim could forget about the list he had seen and even about the young man—mistakes happen all the time—and for a while he could watch eagerly as each candle approached until it became a strange face.

But as the sun set he wasn't waiting for his father any more, just slowly understanding that he wasn't going to see him ever again.

He picked up the head and began to whittle the fine carvings from it, the etchings on the cheeks, the rolling tongue, the nose, the jaw, the eyes . . . . Almost blind with tears, using the knife almost like an axe, Tim was returning the carved head back to a block of wood.

When the last miner came out of the tunnel, Trousselot and another man put on helmets for a final search. A few women stayed round the fires but neither Jean nor Larry spoke much to them.

'One thing, Jean,' Larry said very softly. 'I want to fix it so that the kid never has to become a miner.'

When the two men came out of the mine for the last time, Larry led Jean and Tim slowly down the dark mountain.

# 8

# Home

They spent the rest of the night in a Queenstown hotel and next day returned to Zeehan. There was nothing else they could do.

Tim numbly followed Jean and Larry aboard a different train, driven by a different crew. Jean took his hand as the train pulled away from the station, but they hardly spoke during the long, slow journey. He stared out the window, but could not remember the Abt slopes, or even passing over the Quarter Mile Bridge. Half-way between Strahan and Zeehan he noticed that the carriage seemed to have altered since Queenstown. It was only then that he realized they had changed trains in Strahan.

'All right, kid?' Larry had been watching him for a long time.

'Yeah. S'pose.'

But Larry kept on watching him.

Tim had been remembering things about Dad in the train, the last words on the overland track, his laughter as they'd dammed the creek, the glow in his eyes as he talked about the Thunderer, his last scarred gift—now in a bag between Tim's feet. Every memory hurt but he could not stop them.

And if the train was bad, home was far worse. The corner of an old newspaper lifting from above the kitchen door was a reminder of the way he and Dad had lined the walls. On top of the split paling wall they had put hessian scrim to keep the wind out, then newspaper, then whitewash, making the walls look like plaster. They had finished with so much white over them they 'haunted' the house and Jean for ten glorious minutes.

A creaking floor creaked because Dad had tried to make it level, Tim's knife was sharp because Dad had given him the oilstone, there was a small red mark in the kitchen ceiling because Dad had lost his temper and bounced a stool from the floor to the ceiling, and there was Gran's Room.

The front room, the parlour, had become Gran's Room simply because it contained a photo of Dad's mother. Tim did not like the room, but he was drawn to it now. It was the only room in the house that had wallpaper, bleak brown wallpaper, and normally nobody went in there outside Sunday afternoon. Dad's mother glared down from the mantelpiece from a very black dress and a dusty oval photograph. You got the idea that she knew whatever you'd done and was waiting to punish you for it.

But she was dead—Tim's only other experience of death. Tim had known her only by her letters to Dad from some place in England called Andover. Then the letters stopped coming and Dad didn't want to talk to anyone for a few days, and that was that. Tim stared at the photo and tried to work out what it all meant.

Larry and Jean hunched together in the kitchen for hours, speaking so softly they had to lean on their chairs, Larry examining the back of his fingers, Jean looking away and shaking her head.

Once Jean said, loudly: 'I can't lose him now.'

And Larry said: 'You'll lose him if he stays. Let him work it out.'

Tim caught a few words after that: 'too much of a risk'; 'got to have a chance'; 'can't you leave us alone'; 'not enough jobs'; 'too much to ask'; 'just trust me'. But he couldn't understand any of it.

On the fifth day after the mine disaster Jean called Tim into the kitchen. Larry was looking out the window.

'Been very bad, hasn't it?' Jean sounded flat. She looked at Tim with heavy eyes.

Tim shrugged.

'Larry's going back up the rivers.'

Tim nodded.

'He can take you.'

Tim shook his head. Not now.

'I think you should go.'

'What about the—funeral?'

'They're flooding the mine,' Larry said.

Tim looked from Jean to Larry and back. 'I don't want to go.'

'Oh—' Jean was surprised, but she began to smile. 'Well, all right—'

'No, Jean.' Larry slapped his hand on a drawer. 'Kid, it doesn't matter what you want. It's what you got to do. Your family needs money so you try to step into your Dad's shoes.'

The smile disappeared. 'Larry, I think—'

Larry silenced Jean with a raised finger. 'All right, kid?'

'Ah, yeah.' Tim was looking at the floor.

'Okay. We leave tomorrow morning.'

# The River

# 1

# Rivermen

Two days later Tim was sitting in the stern of a steam launch at the Strahan waterfront, confused and a little frightened. He was watching a nervous Clydesdale draft horse being pushed, pulled and shouted onto a wooden barge by five men. He felt he had a great deal in common with the horse.

Larry jumped into the launch and clapped his hands before Tim's face. 'C'mon, boy, that's enough of the miseries. We got no time.'

The other men leapt into the launch. Two of them were wearing grey flannel coats—blueys—which looked like heavy knee-length nightshirts. But Larry and a thin man were each wearing two flannels, two shirts, one tucked inside the trousers and one hanging loose, and they looked at home in them. All the men were wearing denim dungarees and heavy boots. Tim was wearing a cut-back bluey, looking like one of the men, but feeling like a small boy in someone else's clothes.

The engine revved and began to pull the launch out into the brown water. A heavy rope lifted from the swell, creaked, shook itself clear of water and the barge began to move. The Clydesdale on the barge snorted nervously as two small punts slapped a wave behind him.

Tim remembered the wreck at Trial Harbour and Dad fighting the surf to reach it. He turned away.

'Well, that's that.' Larry turned from the lean man

steering the launch and jerked his thumb at Tim. 'This here's Tim Walker. Kid of Bert, m'brother. He's coming with us.'

A squat man with a bulbous nose and a moustache like a haystack squinted at Tim. 'Why?'

'Why what, Oskar?'

'Why is he here? We run a boys' camp now?'

'Get off it, Oskar.' The thin man with sandy hair was flicking mud from his old felt hat. 'The kid's lost his father.' He turned to Tim with a light smile. 'We're not that bad. I'm Straw.'

But Oskar would not let go. 'Ah, the boy is here because Larry has to baby-sit. I only wanted to know.'

Larry grunted. 'He's going to cook. When he stops sniffling.'

Tim jerked his head up in sudden anger. 'I don't sniffle. Never.'

'Well, that's good,' said Larry. 'Keep it that way.'

Tim jammed his mouth shut and dropped his eyes to the mountain of supplies on the deck of the launch. His bottled rage died in seconds, washed away by a cold dread. He could see large bags of flour, onions, and carrots, cases of tins of cornbeef, mixed meat and herring, saws, axes, chains, block and tackle, rope, tents, huge pots, frying pans, billies . . . . And how much more was there that he couldn't even see? Were they going to go up the rivers for a year? Even longer?

The launch was now out in Macquarie Harbour, a green-brown sea with stark rolling hills lining its rim. Tim pressed his legs together around the single half-empty hessian bag he had brought with him. Everything he knew, Jean, Dad's swimming hole, his vegetable garden, school, Coutts, even Ian, was being left far behind. He was taking only the scarred symbol of Dad, the Huon block, into strange and hostile country and he did not know why.

72

Tim looked back at the mouth of the King River for a last glimpse of familiar country and found himself shaking.

*Number Three* was rocking along the bank, trailing steam across the face of the hills, as if he was seeing himself thundering towards the mine at Queenstown, alive with the certainty of Dad's rescue.

'You'll like it up there, Tim,' Straw said brightly. 'Won't he, Eddy?'

The lined man just nodded once.

Straw smiled. 'We call him Silent Eddy.'

'Oh,' said Tim. 'Why "Silent"?'

'Got nothing to say,' said Silent Eddy.

'He used to be a prospector in the Pilbara,' said Straw. 'That's desert country in Western Australia, and he worked alone.'

Eddy was fifty, hook-nosed, nearly bald, and with a face like an old tree, but for a moment Tim stared at him as if he was looking at a mirror.

The steam launch battered through low waves for several hours, drenching the men and the horse, as massive green mountains loomed above them, heavy grey mist streaming from the peaks. There was no sign of people on the shore, no houses, not even a chopped stump, until waves forced the launch around an island for shelter. An old stone ruin stood alone on a rocky point.

'Remember the cannibals?' Larry said.

Tim blinked. Oh yes, he remembered Larry dropping some lines about the forest when they were after firewood in Zeehan. It surprised him to realize that some things had happened *before* the mine. 'Yes.'

'That's where they come from.'

Tim imagined battle canoes racing from the scrubby shore. He shook his head, but it was good to think of things apart from Dad.

'Larry,' Straw shook his head. 'You're not doing that again.'

'It's true,' Larry said.

Straw sighed. 'Larry would have cannibals swinging from every tree. That's Sarah, or Settlement, Island. Convicts used to build ships there, and it was so bad they'd murder each other or escape. They couldn't find food in the forest so just sometimes they'd eat each other.'

Tim looked at the island again, this time with caution. 'But there's nobody there now. Hasn't been for seventy years. Larry once told Oskar a tale about the cannibals and Oskar wouldn't go to bed that night.'

'Very funny,' muttered Oskar.

Larry turned to Silent Eddy and jerked his thumb at Straw. 'Bloody teacher. Teachers never have fun.'

Tim couldn't help himself. He smiled.

'Tim is not fair game,' Straw said.

'Bull. Stop nursing the kid.'

The waves were dying as the launch approached a flat stretch of brown water between low hills. As the launch dropped speed to enter the river, Tim saw another launch heading toward them. It was towing some logs. No, the launch was towing a riverful of logs. It was towing a raft of six big logs, towing a raft of ten smaller logs, towing another two hundred logs linked together by rope and a very long cable. The moving road of timber curved round a distant bend.

A bearded man in the other launch waved at Larry as the two boats passed each other. 'Beat that, young Larry!'

'Easy, Charlie. Did you break an arm this time?'

The bearded man dismissed Larry with a gesture, but both men were smiling.

'Charlie doesn't come here for logs, y'know,' Larry said. 'He comes here to explore. He's been just about everywhere.'

'And if he hasn't been everywhere he'll do it next year,' Straw said. The men in the launch laughed and even Oskar smiled.

The Gordon narrowed as thick, dark forest reared from its banks to disappear in floating mist. Tim could hear the

74

rattle of chains and the dull *chonk!* of axes biting into wood echoing on the water but he couldn't see anything. The engine of the steam launch seemed to sound deeper and louder.

'Well, here's where I drop you, Larry,' the skipper of the launch said. ''Course I could take you as far as The Big Eddy tomorrow.'

The launch turned with the river towards a roughly-built landing stage where a man was waiting with rope coiled over his shoulder. The Clydesdale pulled at its halter.

'Thanks Frank, but we'll best be goin'.' Larry stood up.

The barge was manoeuvred near the landing and then pushed into place. The man with the rope stepped onto the punt.

''Ow'd he go?' he said, then recognized Larry. 'Sorry about your brother, mate.'

'It happens. Brought his kid along.'

'Best thing.' The man with the rope nuzzled the horse and led it ashore while Eddy and Oskar loaded two of the punts.

Tim watched the Clydesdale plod up the hill with a little sorrow, as if a friend was leaving. 'What's the horse for?'

'Pulling logs,' Straw said. 'They've found a stand of Huon way up Fawkes Creek. They need horses to get the logs to the river, and that one makes up a team. There's a lot of trees there and there are a lot of men up there. Even somebody's wife.'

Tim could smell a rich stew in the air and he saw a few shacks through the trees. 'We don't have any horses.'

'No. We use a block and tackle and our own backs. If it's too big or too far from the river we just leave it be.'

'It looks like a whole village of piners.' Tim wanted to go ashore and eat.

Straw laughed. 'Not quite a village. Just a few huts.

75

Oh, and we don't call ourselves piners. Piners are people that used to do what we do, anywhere but here.'

'Yeah,' Larry grunted. 'We are really special.' And for a moment Tim thought he was going to laugh.

'Well, maybe we are,' said Straw. 'Tim, we are River-men. We go into country right off the map. We go up the wild rivers, the Gordon, the Franklin, the Denison, the Jane, the Maxwell, and nobody knows what it's like but us.'

Larry nodded at the black water. 'They're still all cold, rough—and too much hard work. Let's go.'

Oskar and Eddy got into one punt without a word to each other and rowed away, a four-legged beetle scudding across the water. Larry and Straw waited for Tim in the other punt.

Tim jumped from the launch and rocked the low punt dangerously.

'Hell, boy, use your head!' Larry steadied the punt with an oar.

'Sorry.'

'You'd be sorry all right if you'd capsized the boat. You'd be the one that wouldn't eat.'

'Hey, Larry, ease off,' Straw said. 'He's only a boy.'

'No. Back there, he's a boy. He can play smart tricks on his mates and sneak off to ride trains. Back there. Here we got no room at all for boys.'

Larry rowed strongly up the black Gordon.

# 2

# The Convict's Hut

Late in the afternoon the sky cleared, turning the dark river into a polished mirror. Ahead of Tim's punt the river became the sky, with motionless trees reaching for the depths. A pale yellow flower bent from the bank to kiss its twin sister as the punt passed over a small white cloud. For a while Tim felt that *he* was under the water, looking up at the punt, the trees and the sky. But the image dissolved when he looked back. The oars were leaving a chain of widening circles in the river and the punts were sending ripples to the banks, distorting the trees captured in the water.

Tim dried and warmed in the sun. He trailed a finger in the water and found that if he closed his eyes enough to see through his lashes he could almost persuade himself that Straw was Dad. Dad was pulling on the oars, his eyes glinting under the broad brim of the hat, and the mine was no more than last night's bad dream.

'You know why the Gordon's black?' Straw said, as he leant back from the oar. And Dad shimmered and dissolved.

Tim shook his head, wishing that Straw would shut up and change back.

But Straw could not be stopped. 'It's the only one that is. The Franklin, the Jane, the Denison, the rivers that flow into the Gordon, they're all brown. Not muddy brown, but tea-brown from the roots of the button grass.

This river's so black it works like a photographic plate, reflecting everything above it. But the blackness is only from the button grass stain and it tastes lovely. The secret is the depth.'

Tim gave up and opened his eyes. He remembered the crimson streams he'd seen in the button grass country of Zeehan. They were only a few inches deep, but they were as red as a sunset. If they were deep, like Big Henty, they were brown. But this river?

'The Gordon is maybe 120 feet deep in parts. It carries more water than any other river in Tasmania and it runs quietly all the time.'

'Almost,' said Larry. 'Now stop prattling to the kid and pull.'

They rowed up the Gordon until long shadows crept from the bank, then pulled towards an old hut, its walls green with moss.

Larry stopped rowing and leant towards Tim. 'Okay kid, it's your act.' The punt slid to a staggered landing.

'What?' Tim looked at Larry guardedly. He didn't know what Larry was talking about, but it meant trouble.

'In that hut there's a fireplace.' Larry shipped his oar.

'Yes?'

'Get a fire going and cook us some dinner.'

'Oh.' Tim looked at the hut. He did not like it at all. The rusting corrugated iron roof was bearing down on a chimney of blackened palings and sagging split-log walls. The hut looked as if it was about to collapse. It looked bleak, damp and dangerous. 'Just by myself?'

'That's what you're here for. Get on with it.'

Straw started to say something, then caught Larry's eye and concentrated on laying his oar in the punt.

Tim grabbed his bag and leapt angrily ashore. He strode into the hut swinging the bag like a club and was immediately covered with a spider's web. He spluttered, stopped, clawed the sticky threads from his eyes and tried to see.

78

The hut smelt of rotting wood and wet charcoal, and looked like a bear's cave. Tim could see an open fireplace set in a tumble of scorched rocks, a low stack of chopped wood with water dripping onto it, and stacked bunks with mouldering ferns hanging from the boards.

He dropped his sack with a thump, picked up a log that was heavy with water and realized that he was carrying no matches, no paper, nothing he could use to start the fire. And even if he had everything, he still couldn't burn these damp logs.

Tim stood in the middle of the hut and silently damned Larry for dragging him from home into this miserable place, for treating him all the time like a stupid brat, and finally for giving him work to do that was impossible. Impossible so he can't do it, proving he's a stupid brat . . . . You can't win.

'It's a dump, isn't it?' Straw had pushed into the hut behind Tim. He dumped a sack and scratched his jaw with his axe. But he was smiling.

Tim nodded helplessly.

'Don't worry, it looks better with a fire on. Crumple a page of the newspaper in m'bag and clear out the chimney.' Straw took the log from Tim, set it on the ground and split it.

While Tim prepared the fireplace he watched Straw squat before the split log and reduce it to a pile of fine kindling, rocking the axe head to a finger's width from his retreating fingertips.

Tim could make a fire now, and when Straw threw him a box of matches he made the kindling crackle in the fireplace in half a minute.

Straw split two other logs; they were very dry inside. 'It's a very old hut,' Straw said, as smoke billowed into the hut. 'It started as a convict hut—maybe Goodwyn's— then the rivermen took over. Don't worry, the chimney'll draw when the fire gets hot.'

Tim coughed. 'Who's Goodwyn?'

'He was one of the few convicts who escaped. And he didn't eat anybody either. He got sick of sending logs down to Sarah Island so he and a mate hoarded their food, stole a punt and went up the Franklin. Listen, don't let them get you. Just give us some fresh food before it goes off.' Straw winked and walked outside to help the others.

Tim felt the fire's heat growing on his back and smiled. Impossible, eh? Stupid brat, eh? He'd show that thick plank of an uncle, he would.

He built the fire into a steady red glow with almost no flames as Straw and Eddy brought the supplies in from the punts. He found some chuck steak, diced it, rolled it in flour, fried it briefly and threw it into simmering water in the great pot as the basis for a stew. He tried to find the salt, failed, but swept out the hut with a branch and felt in control of things.

Then the rain and Oskar came together.

The rain swept over the hut as Tim dropped peeled potatoes, chopped onions and sliced carrots into the stew. The roof creaked and roared and water dribbled into the hut in a dozen places. The fire spluttered and black drops skidded down the chimney and into the stew until Tim slammed the lid on.

Oskar, Larry and Eddy strode into the hut, grunting, water pouring from their shoulders, carrying the last of stores from the punts and freshly-chopped wood.

'Where is dinner?' Oskar glared at Tim.

Tim was happy with how things were going and shrugged casually. 'Not ready yet.'

'Why is it not ready now? I am hungry now.'

'I'm making a stew. It needs an hour.'

'Hour?' Oskar dumped a bag and hauled Tim into the air, almost touching the boy's face with his own dripping moustache. 'Hour?' he thundered, his eyes catching the flames from the fireplace, his cheeks turning dark red. 'You maybe want me to die of hunger?'

80

Tim squirmed and thought: this bloke's mad, crazy as a parrot. Why don't they haul him off me, before he gets serious?

Then he looked round and hung loose. Larry was watching without making any movement to save him, as if he was just wondering what was going to happen. Eddy was rubbing his nose.

'Well, boy?' Oskar roared.

Tim swallowed. 'Well, you could eat it now—'

Oskar dropped Tim back on the floor. 'That is better,' he said and lumbered over to the pot.

'But it would taste better later.'

Oskar stopped. 'Taste?'

'And you'd find most of the vegetables raw.' Tim backed towards the door.

Oskar took a step from the pot, but stopped with a shrug. 'Hokay. I wait. But maybe we roast smart little boy later, eh?'

'Kid, you find Straw and bring him in,' Larry said. He seemed to be fighting a smile. 'Anyone for a cup of tea?'

Tim found Straw outside the hut examining a perfect row of tiny trees less than a pace from the side wall.

'Who planted these Huon pines?' he asked in astonishment.

Straw smiled. 'Nobody. The seeds were dropped in the corrugations of the hut's roof about three years ago, then the rain washed them down the grooves to plant them in a line. Like them?'

'Pretty good.'

'I saw your whittling block. Do you do much work on Huon?'

'When I can get hold of it.'

'You're in the right spot now.' Straw shook his head. 'Huon's my favourite tree, so I spend my time chopping down Huons. How's that? Let's go inside.'

81

* * *

Tim awoke in the blackness of early morning as the fragments of a warm dream slid from him. He had been boiling a mutton bird on the rocky headland overlooking the wreck and Dad was waist deep in the flashing white foam below. For a moment a curling wave had swept over him but it left him riding the great wooden figurehead, laughing and waving . . . .

Then he'd gone, and Tim was cold and alone beside a dead fire. He tried to slither back into the dream, failed and realized with a slight shock that he had not thought of Dad at all since yesterday afternoon. There had been too much to do. He felt guilty for a while, then the guilt had curdled into something else.

Dad should be here.

Larry yawned and got the rivermen on their feet.

Dad should not have got a job in the mine. He should have known. Nobody asked him to go into the mine, nobody needed him there . . . .

The rivermen finished the stew, loaded the punts, and left the hut with the rickety chimney and the line of marching trees for a silent and sinister river.

'What's the trouble, Tim?'

'Nothing.'

It's not much to ask, is it? Just to look after yourself for a month. But not him, oh no, never. Go out to an old wreck through surf that is tearing it apart, just to see if you can save a great wooden mermaid? Oh, sure. Go to the bottom of a mine just before it is filled with poison gas, just to see if you can get out? Oh, sure.

The Gordon was now covered in mist, a mist so dense it blocked the sun from the water and the banks from the punts. Tim was screwing a fist into his palm, staring at Straw as he rowed easily and alone without apparently touching the water. He would dip his blade in the mist, the mist would swirl and flow over the hafts, there would be a gentle gurgle and the blades would rise from the mist, that was all. They could be anywhere now; on a river, on a lake, or in the middle of the ocean. They couldn't see anything, they couldn't hear anything, they couldn't tell.

Tim huddled in the stern of the boat, and shivered, and thought. He's let us all down. Me, Jean, Ian, even Larry. Why did he have to do it?

'It'll improve,' Straw smiled at Tim.

'It'll have to,' Larry threatened the river from the bow.

Tim heard muffled thuds somewhere ahead but ignored them.

'What's up, Tim?' Straw looked up.

'I don't know.'

A tall shadow began to grow in the mist.

Straw stopped rowing and frowned. 'What's that?'

The thuds became rapid blows as the shadow developed into an immense block in the water, with sheer sides and a bow cutting towards the punts.

Tim jerked upright, Dad and the mine swept from him in a terrifying instant. 'It's a ship!'

'Bloody pirates,' muttered Larry.

# 3

# Pirates!

Tim looked up at the black hull and tensed himself to jump into the water. The ship would be on them in a handful of seconds. A pirate ship?

But Larry and Straw were totally ignoring it.

'You reckon?' said Straw, and actually stopped paddling.

'You wouldn't chop trees down here,' Larry muttered. 'They're pirates all right.'

Tim tugged at Larry's sleeve and pointed frantically at the ship.

'Yeah kid, Butler Island. Get Oskar in, Straw.'

Tim looked back at the ship and saw that it wasn't really moving and it had a tree growing out from the hull. It was no more than a tall island of grey rock sitting in the middle of the Gordon. It looked like a ship only if you were daft enough to believe a ship could, or would, come this far up the river.

But Larry had been serious about the pirates, and still was.

Oskar and Eddy slid silently out of the mist behind Straw and turned towards him.

'Pirates?' whispered Oskar.

Larry nodded.

'We get 'em, eh?' Eddy looked very happy.

'Yeah,' said Larry. 'Keep it quiet. Tim, you get hold of the punts when we hit the sand. Right?'

Tim nodded his head and saw with a shock the fear in Oskar's eyes. This wasn't a joke like the cannibals, this was real and Dad should be here to tell everyone what to do.

As the punts moved toward the steady chopping sound Tim strained to see through the mist, imagining giants with long curved blades. He wanted Larry to change his mind, to turn their tiny punts and row quietly down the river, but the sounds from the shore were getting louder with every stroke.

The punts moved into a lazy swirl of water to the right of Butler Island and followed a chain of logs, a boom, from the island to the shore. Shadowy figures were moving on the shore, one swinging in time with the chopping sound, and three more pulling something from the river. There were two punts pulled up to the bank a little downstream.

Tim was frightened. He was so frightened the hairs on his legs were curling away from the skin and his throat was clogging. It wasn't fair to shove a tiny kid into a situation like this, to set him up with lovely stories about exploring great rivers, finding mythical waterfalls—and then to leave him alone in a nightmare. It just wasn't fair!

'Tim,' Straw was swinging his body forward and back, driving the oars in great arcs just above the water. He spoke softly only when his head was close to Tim. 'You okay?'

And now they were going to make out he was a baby. Well all right!

Tim nodded, but he jammed his legs together and clenched his fists.

The chopping stopped. The three shadows dropped something half into the water and backed nervously away from the river.

Larry stood in the bow of the punt with his axe in his hands, took a mighty step to the bank, and bellowed.

For one instant the shadows were close enough to

become men, one with an axe, the others with hooks, all wearing blueys and beards. Then the roar of a mad bull echoed along the still valley and a giant was running at them with a horde of angry men behind him. The pirates dropped their tools, turned and fled.

And Tim leapt from his punt with an oar held over his head. He screamed at the pirates as he ran past the jogging Straw and Eddy, past Larry and hurled the oar at the last disappearing pirate.

He stared at the bush, hearing the pirates blundering and tumbling in the steep forest and the rivermen talking behind him without moving. He was trembling.

Straw clapped his hand on Tim's shoulder. 'Well, we sure taught them a lesson, eh?'

Tim stood with tightly-balled fists at his sides.

'Log pirates, Tim,' Straw said. 'We cut trees up river and push them into the river if we can. If we can't, we just leave them where the winter floods will bring them down. Either way we brand them so we know the logs are ours. But these low lads pinch them.'

'These bludgers.' Larry showed Straw a hammer with a something like a raised J in a circle on the striking face of the head.

'See, Tim?' Straw thumbed over his shoulder at the chained logs. 'They string a boom anywhere to catch our logs, chop off our brands and put on their own brand.'

'Hell, the punt!' Larry roared, dropping the hammer beside Straw. He hurled himself into the river after the two rapidly drifting punts.

Straw whistled a single note in regret; then he saw that Tim had not moved. He was still staring at the forest, trembling and with his fists tight by his sides. He did not seem to be aware of Larry swimming wildly after the punts.

'What's up, mate?' Straw said sharply.

'I hate him,' Tim said.

'Who, Larry?'

Tim shook his head. 'Dad.'

# 4

# The Franklin

Larry emerged dripping from the river with the punts in tow and fury washing over his face. He started to tell Tim just what sort of a stupid, cloth-headed, twit of a boy he was, but Straw managed to catch his eye. Larry stopped his attack on Tim but took his temper out on the log pirates. He pitched their hammer into the middle of the river, cut the boom adrift and put his axe through the bottom of both of the pirates' punts. He towed them as the rivermen rowed upstream until they sank and only then began to smile.

'They are going to have a hell of a walk home,' he said happily, as he shrugged out of his sodden outer flannel.

But as Larry brightened, Tim slipped deeper into misery. Until now, he had had the warmth of anger to keep out the slow hurt, but he had thrown that away with the oar. Now he had to sit in the stern of the boat and think of what he had thought, done and said on this misty morning. He spent most of the morning wishing for icy rain, floods, black rapids, anything to make him feel he was being punished enough.

But by the time the punts reached the Franklin river the mist had been sucked up by a bright sun, and the high dark hills had rolled back from the Gordon, allowing a breeze to rustle the leaves of trees over the water. Larry, still wearing the dungarees and flannel from the swim, was beginning to steam.

They rowed toward a small sandy island sitting smugly where the Franklin met the solemn Gordon with a shimmy and a bounce.

'Now we have to work,' Larry said.

Larry and Straw, rowing fast, were able to move slowly against the flashing water, but they had to wait for fifteen minutes for Eddy and Oskar to leave Pyramid Island behind them.

'Still worrying about the punts that got away?' Straw smiled.

'He ought to,' growled Larry.

'No, the other thing.' Tim was staring at Larry. If Larry knew what he had said . . . .

'What other thing?' Larry asked.

'Probably the mine,' said Straw quickly. 'Here come the others.'

Soon the river became very broad, shallow and fast. The water became white and bumpy, scouring the sides of the punts as it giggled past. Larry and Straw could still creep past the heavy trees on the bank by rowing furiously and shouting at each other, but Larry looked sideways to see Oskar's punt smoothly passing them and missed a stroke in surprise.

Oskar and Eddy had abandoned ship and were wading.

'March, march, march!' Oskar bellowed at Eddy. Eddy looked as if he were about to let go of the punt and go for Oskar's throat, but the two men were surging ahead.

'What the hell—' Larry sighed and jumped into the river. It was knee deep. Straw followed him.

Tim could see the smooth shingles on the bottom through the tea-coloured water but decided against joining them. He was too short to help. Larry would probably shout him out of the water, and he was no good anyway. He hunched in the stern of the punt and watched the banks slowly pass by. Bushes reached out to trail their prickly foliage in the rushing water, and wind-scoured trees with heavy crowns leant perilously over the punt.

Tim felt that some tall trees, catching a patch of wind, were shaking their heads at him.

But soon the river stopped. The forest on both sides became almost flat and the water was like glass. Grey limestone cliffs had been carved by the river in flood to create a crowd of bizarre stone faces.

'The Verandah Cliffs,' said Straw to Tim. 'Look there.'

He was pointing at a hunk of wood, big as a man, punched through a column of rock twenty feet above the river.

'That was done by a flood in winter.'

But Tim was not interested.

Larry made camp round the next bend. He asked Tim to tie the punts, then checked the knots. Tim cooked steak and eggs with a billy of black tea. Even Oskar could not complain, but Tim would have almost welcomed the abuse.

Straw caught Tim after dinner. 'How you feeling now?'

'Lousy.'

'Still hate your dad?'

'No.' Tim looked away. 'I dunno . . . I hate *me*.'

'Look, it's all right. Really. I came to the rivers when my wife and daughter died almost together, died, you know that? Died of diphtheria. Just for a bit I thought that was very selfish of Helen, my wife, dying like that. But you get over it.'

Next day Tim got up before the others. He stoked the fire into life and put the billy on and went for a quick swim in the icy river, gasping, whistling and singing a word or two. He could remember every bleak moment of yesterday morning; but yesterday was yesterday and somehow he was different. He did not even want to go home any more.

After a breakfast of bacon and eggs, during which Oskar told Tim to cut the insufferable whistling, the punts were loaded and launched. Soon Tim could hear a low rumble from the river ahead.

'Big Fall,' said Straw. 'It can kill you. We get out and walk.'

The entire river roared down a rocky cleft and dropped into a boiling cauldron of white water. Oskar and Eddy joined Larry and Straw on a flat rock and the four men carried the first punt slowly round the fall while Tim looked after the second punt.

During a rest in carrying the second punt, Tim stood on a water-carved rock and looked down at a small rainbow over the fall. He felt the spray on his face and the thunder in his head as the streaked water drove deep into the bucking foam. He was enjoying the channelled power of the river when he began to see something terrible in the water . . .

'Some trickle, eh, kid?' Larry had walked up behind him.

Tim turned, and lost the image in the water. 'Yeah. Suppose.'

Larry looked at the fall, at Tim, and at the fall again. He seemed awkward, as if he was trying to say something but did not know how. 'Gets better as we go upstream.'

Tim nodded.

'Good breakfast.'

'Thanks.'

'It's not going to be so bad. Better than home. Too much to do to think about it all the time.'

Tim breathed out heavily. 'Miss Dad,' he said, and closed a door on the pirate's beach.

'We all do.'

Tim looked up in surprise. He had forgotten that the huge bad-tempered man was Dad's brother. Maybe he felt a little sad about everything too. Tim swept aside the startled expression and started to share his feelings.

But Larry had read Tim's face and hardened again. 'But you want to watch yourself, kid. You're too damned close to the fall.'

Tim stepped back and tried to speak again.

'That water would kill you.'

Tim forgot what he was about to say. 'I can swim good,' he protested.

Larry picked up a thick hunk of wood and threw it into the cauldron. It disappeared. A little later it bobbed to the surface nearer to the fall but it disappeared again a moment later. 'These falls won't let go, kid. If you're stupid enough to get caught in one, you don't swim, you go for the bottom to get out. I don't want to go to Jean and tell her that you've gone as well.'

'The bottom?' Tim asked, but Larry strode away.

He watched the piece of wood come again, go again, and saw the image in the water again. Not brown water plunging deep in a mist of bubbles but the long black shaft of a mine, not the trapped fragment of a branch but a man struggling desperately to escape.

What had it been like? Up there the jammed cages and the fire pumping gas into the levels, down here the candles flickering, and the air tasting bad, and nowhere to go . . . .

'Come on, Tim,' called Straw.

After a couple of hours fighting the river Larry had seen the light, spidery foliage of several Huon pines in the forest and made for the bank. The punts were pulled well up on the bank, the men cleared a small area between two massive myrtles and Tim lugged, or dragged, the bags and tools from the punts. Two tents were pitched facing each other with a fly stretched between them. Tim was going to do most of his cooking under the fly. The punts were carried from the river, upended and used as shelters for tools and tins.

Larry emerged from a tent in a dry shirt and a patched waistcoat and nodded at Tim. 'That's better, eh?' He tightened the cords that ran round each dungaree leg below the knee.

Tim frowned. 'What's that?'

91

'Bowyangs. Keeps the odd leech out. Well, how'd'you like your new home?'

'Home?'

'Maybe for a month or so. Until we get the logs down to the river.'

'It's all right,' Tim said flatly. It was all right, sometimes it was a bit of fun, when they were moving. See what that strange sound around the next bend is, dodge that soggy log, watch that mountain change. But if they were here there was nothing to think about but Dad. He did not want to think about Dad any more.

'It can be all right,' Larry said. 'It's up to you.'

But after dinner the rivermen went off to inspect trees, leaving Tim alone by the low fire to wash the dishes and listen to the silence of the forest. He could lean against the mossy bole of the leaning myrtle near his tent, listening to the murmur of the river and maybe the sway of a tree. He could look into the forest, the tall trees jostling each other for sunlight, the ferns open and ready for rain, the bright green moss covering the ground like a rich carpet. But he could neither see nor hear anything living. As if everything was waiting.

Tim left the fire, picked up his bag and walked to the river for something to do. He sat on a rock and fished in his bag as the setting sun warmed his face. He found his oil stone and began honing his knife, the old familiar rhythm relaxing him.

He supposed it wasn't all that bad.

The blade flickered brightly as the golden touch of day slowly lifted from the Elliot range. He could hear the river rippling far away. He watched the insects lazily drifting over the water and yawned.

He wondered how Jean and Ian were going. Was she cleaning up the Blood House as usual? Was Ian crawling about the place, looking for him? No, the only time Ian ever noticed him was when he wanted something to bite.

They ought to put him on a leash. Jean would be missing him; and he missed her. But just now not so much.

The water swirled near his arm.

'Fish?' he asked the river, reaching for the Huon block in the bag.

Something like a fur glove broke the water and looked at him.

'Beat it,' he said, afraid for a moment.

He saw the broad, black beak, a webbed foot, then the platypus slid smoothly to the bottom.

Tim stared at the water and began to smile.

But then he looked at the scarred block in his right hand and remembered how and where it had received those scars. He stopped smiling, drew back his arm and hurled the block far into the river.

'Leave me alone,' he told the river.

# 5

# Tracks

The river did. Larry did not.

Tim was still sitting on the rock when the camp behind him erupted in a confusion of shouting and thrashing, as if a dozen men were fighting an elephant.

The pirates! Tim thought as he ran towards the camp.

But the rivermen were beating at a smoking black circle round the hissing fire with their flannels. Larry was kicking a burning branch away from a smouldering tent corner when he saw Tim.

'Boy!' His booming roar echoed in the forest. Tim very nearly turned and ran. 'What the hell did you think you were doing? Eh? Haven't you got a single brain in your head?'

'Ah—' Tim swallowed. 'I just wanted to watch the river—'

'You *what*? You just—' And Larry took a great step to Tim and clipped him across the ear with an open hand.

Tim reeled sideways, stumbled and fell with a roaring in his head. Larry was still shouting at him, but for a few seconds he could not hear the words.

'—leave you to look after the camp and you just about burn us out. Maybe even burn this whole forest out. Everything. First it's the punts, now this. By God, if you do anything else like this you get put on a log to paddle yourself home. I mean it.'

'Larry?' Straw was standing by the leaning myrtle, fingering the bark.

'You're not protecting the kid again?'

'Not this time.' Tim felt his body sag. Straw wasn't even looking at him. 'Have a look.'

Larry walked to the tree and followed Straw's finger to a root and up the trunk. 'Tiger?' he said.

'I think so,' said Straw.

'Wouldn't have spread the fire.'

'Probably not. Still, we'll have to watch.'

'Not us. Him.' Larry nodded at Tim. 'Hear that, kid? You make sure you're awake when the tiger comes.'

\* \* \*

Next morning Tim cooked a breakfast of thick burgoo, bacon and potatoes, washed the dishes while the rivermen went to their trees, and examined the leaning myrtle in the bright morning light.

It took him ten minutes to find anything at all on the smooth green trunk, a fingernail of lifted bark here, an almost invisible puncture there, a slight scratch level with his head. But his spine prickled when he saw part of a paw mark in the mud near a root. No longer than his thumb, but it was as menacing as a single eye in a dark bush.

He stalked about the camp for most of the morning with his eyes roving over the silent undergrowth and the high branches. He took some comfort in the sounds of the rivermen working, the slashing of machetes, the slow rhythm of axes and the rasp of the two-man saw, and he took lunch to the men half an hour early. He stopped in a shadowed hollow when a man shouted, and spilled tea from his billy as a tree crashed to the ground. He ran under some spreading manferns and over a rotting log to the safety of the men.

The tree lay towards Tim's path through the forest,

with the men chopping away the branches and crown. The tree had not been big, perhaps no more than forty feet tall, and it was being reduced to a straight log, thirty feet long and no broader than Tim's body.

'Lunch!' Tim shouted. He deliberately lowered his voice to hide the quiver.

'Any sign of the tiger?' Larry said, grabbing a handful of sandwiches.

'Nah,' Tim said, as if it did not worry him at all. He poured tea for Straw.

'Thanks Tim,' Straw said, leaning on the stump of the newly-felled Huon. 'How's the fire?'

The fire, not the tiger. 'It's all right. I dug a proper pit. Ah—' Tim looked up at Straw, his only friend out here and maybe not a friend any more. 'You real mad at me?'

Straw pushed his hat back. 'Just don't let it happen again. Maybe the tiger knocked something over, but it shouldn't have been able to. We can't afford the risk.'

'Yeah, I suppose.'

'Tim, I don't think you know what a fire could do here. This is myrtle rain forest, slow growing. It's never seen a fire for hundreds of years and it won't cope with one now. A fire could wipe out the slow rain forest trees, the myrtles, the pines, and the fast trees, the Eucalypts, would take over. The forest would change and never change back. And then you'd probably kill the Huons.'

'But they're supposed to be instructable.'

'Indestructible. Almost, but not quite.' Straw picked up a chip from the stump. 'You ever chew the wood?'

Tim wrinkled his nose. 'Just once.' He had scraped his tongue with fingernails to get rid of the harshly bitter taste.

Straw smiled. 'It's enough, isn't it? That's the horrible secret. No insect or fungus or disease can ever attack Huon pine with that defence in the sap, so it lasts for ever. You build a boat of Huon and it could still be sailing a thousand years from now. And the sap is good for

96

toothache and treating injuries. It doesn't burn well, but I don't think it would stand up all that well in a forest fire.'

Tim hunched his shoulders and changed the subject. 'That why you come all the way up here for them? Knew the wood was good, but I didn't know it was *that* good.'

'We still don't know just how good it is. Trouble is it's a slow grower. Maybe the slowest grower of them all. For instance, this tree, how old do you reckon?'

Tim looked at the width and length of the fallen tree and glanced at the rings on the stump, one ring of wood for every year of growth. 'Forty years,' he said.

Straw spilled his tea over the flat, sawn part of the tree. 'Now count the rings again,' he said.

Under the tea the wood glowed lemon with the fine, dark rings dancing round the stump less than a hair's breadth apart.

Tim was still counting when the rivermen finished lunch and went back to work. Oskar and Eddy sawed the trunk into two equal lengths while Larry and Straw fitted a metal 'shoe' to the downhill end of the trunk. The shoe would act as a ski tip, lifting the end of the log from the ground as it was hauled. 'Dogs'—iron rings—were hammered into the wood to hold the shoe in place and to take the ends of heavy chains, and ropes were connected to the chains.

'Three hundred and nineteen,' Tim said faintly.

'What?' said Larry.

'Years', said Straw. 'That's how old this tree is. A little older than Guy Fawkes.'

'Only a sapling,' said Larry.

'Yeah. Only a sapling. The good big trees are far older, Tim. Out here a fire doesn't just burn trees. It burns centuries.'

★ ★ ★

97

Tim worked solidly in camp the next day, almost without looking at the spreading branches over his head. He used some light cord and sticks to build a wash stand and dish rack and enlarged gutter trenches round the tents while the second log was hauled down to the river. Tomorrow he would rig up a clothes line, spread bark around the tents to cover the mud and maybe see what he could do with his knife. To his surprise he was beginning to enjoy the camp, the forest and the river, but occasionally—just occasionally—he would amble over to the leaning myrtle and look at the paw mark.

After lunch Larry picked up his branding hammer from a tent and pointed at Tim's work. 'What's that?'

'A washstand,' Tim said proudly.

'We'll have to give you something to do.'

Larry walked to the two logs, swung the hammer twice, threw it into the tent and went back into the forest.

Tim straightened from the trench he had been digging and threw down the shovel. He went to his washstand and shook it.

'What's wrong with it?' he called, a little too softly to be heard.

'Eh?' Louder this time. He ran to the logs and kicked hard at the brand. And stopped.

A deep circle with a 'W' in the pale lemon wood. 'W' for Walker. Dad.

Tim turned away. It was like the river, like the dreams, like the house. They won't ever let go . . . .

Then Tim turned back and frowned. This time it still hurt, but not as much. He could think of Albert Walker now without some sort of clogging in his throat. Walker was Albert, Dad, not him, not Larry—and Larry should not pinch the initial for a dead log.

Tim thought as he pulled a great hunk of salt beef from the food store.

And he shouldn't try to pinch his kid. He wasn't good enough for that.

Tim dunked the salt beef in a pot full of water and glared at it.

There was all the world of difference between Albert and Larry. With Dad you were mates. Sure, he told you what to do, but he listened when you wanted to talk about things. Sometimes—like in the swimming hole— he even followed your ideas and you were king of the world after that. Often you'd make mistakes, but that was okay because he'd make mistakes too and he'd laugh. When he was around you'd do great things together.

But with Larry you were the stupid kid. He was the big-time explorer of the wilderness and he never made mistakes, never needed anyone. All you could do was try to be as good as him so he'd have to leave you alone. Like a kid. Like *his* kid.

Not good enough. Show him you're Albert's kid, show him that you can do anything at all.

Tim sluiced the water in the pot. He would leave the meat for two hours before cooking to get rid of some of the salt—and why not cut his own firewood while he waited? He picked up one of the lighter axes and strode along the bank of the river.

He found two dead sassafras saplings hanging over the river a hundred yards downstream from the camp, and was swinging at the trunk of one when something bobbing in the water caught his eye.

Dad's last gift to him, the scarred block, nodded at him from a slow eddy. It bobbed against a tumbled log, grinned and rocked away.

Tim hesitated, then dropped the axe and waded into the river. He smoothed the water from the face and turned it from him.

'Okay Dad,' he said softly.

He returned to the camp with the block sitting on top of the pile of wood in his arms.

But the tiger had arrived.

# 6

# Tiger

The big pot was on its side in a puddle of spilled water, still rolling back and forth.

'Hey!' Tim shouted and dropped his logs.

The pot kept rolling.

Tim hurled a light log at the pot, catching it with a ringing clang and curling it into the air.

Something leapt backwards from the pot, brown and white spots, all claws and bared teeth. Hissing like a boiler about to burst.

Tim hesitated.

The animal shrieked in fury, flattened his ears and ran at him.

Tim screamed and bolted back into the forest.

He stopped clawing his way through a tangled mass of ferns and shrubbery when he realized the animal was not at his heels. He stopped, leant against a tree until the trembling passed then crept slowly back into the camp with a heavy branch in his hands. The animal was gone, and so was the salt beef.

Tim mixed a thick paste of flour, salt and water to make a damper, then opened tins of herring and tomato sauce and waited for Larry. He sat on one of the Huon logs and wondered how he was going to paddle it home.

But Larry was surprisingly calm about the whole thing. 'You lost all of it? Four pounds of beef?'

'Yes . . . it was awful wild. With huge claws and fangs—you've never seen anything like it.'

'Yeah, a tiger. A tiger cat. Suppose we ought to be happy you didn't see a tiger dog. How big was it?'

Tim wanted to tell Larry that his tiger cat was as big as a real Indian tiger, bigger than Larry, big enough to carry him away in his mouth. But it wasn't and Larry would never believe him. 'It was bigger than a cat—' He held up his hands two feet apart. 'Lots bigger than a cat. Maybe it was really a tiger dog, after all.'

Straw shook his head. 'No, you wouldn't see a thylacine. Not here.'

'It was big—'

'But not as big as a thylacine. Look, these Tasmanian tigers are only some sort of striped wild dog, frightened to blazes of people. Just a whiff of you would scare a thylacine two miles off and there aren't many of them left now. No, you saw a tiger cat.'

'A small tiger cat,' said Larry.

'Ah, not all that small, Larry,' Straw said. 'It took away four pounds of meat; quite a mouthful.'

'Sure. I'm not blaming the kid. That cat might be hard to handle for such a little boy. Let's forget it.'

\* \* \*

Tim was frightened as he wandered through the camp, but Larry's casual goad pricked him like a burr. Now he was not only stupid and careless, he was too much a small boy to be any good, any time. Leave him in the safe schoolyard, he's useless anywhere else. That hurt far more than the clip across the head.

He *had* to stop the tiger next time.

For two days Tim looked for the cat in the tents, under the punts, behind the wood pile and in every tree he walked under. For a while he felt like Sheriff Jim heading

102

for the showdown, then he realized that if he saw the tiger he still didn't know what to do.

He squatted by the fire, slowly removed the scars from Dad's block, and hoped that the tiger would not return.

At the end of the first week the men left their clearing for a Sunday off. They got up an hour later, washed their clothes and built stretcher beds out of some of the empty sacks and straight saplings. They sharpened their axes, sewed the rips in their blueys and Larry, Straw and Oskar played a little poker while Silent Eddy looked vainly for gold traces in the river. As the sun sank over the Elliot range, Larry walked back to the clearing and beyond. When he came back he looked unhappy.

'It still looks big,' he said.

'Corduroy track?'

'And tackle. The whole box of tricks. And I don't know if we can move it, even then.'

'Leave it until last.'

Larry shrugged.

Straw caught the question in Tim's eye. 'We've got a monster up there. It's a lovely tree, but we don't know if we can bring it down.'

Tim was asked to chop more wood than he needed, and to bring any lopped branches more than three feet long to the clearing. Wooden pulleys and more rope were taken to the clearing but the work was slowing down. One tree fell with a crash that Tim could feel through his boots, and the first log from the tree took two days to reach the river.

But Tim was in no hurry. He had taken the block to the river one afternoon, washed it under the eye of a curious big-beaked currawong, and seen a new shape under the wood. The block developed a bumpy ridge and suddenly started guiding the blade in his fingers.

He was turning the block in his hands as he walked into the store tent when the tent hissed.

103

He tumbled outside and rose to one knee to see two amber jewels glinting at him from a fallen sack.

'Oh boy,' he breathed. His feet wanted to run but he pressed them into the ground.

Remember, it's only a cat. Just a bad-tempered cat.

Tim scrambled to his feet and the cat made a sound like a strangled roar in his throat. The fangs were glistening.

He backed away from the tent and snagged his clothes on his dish rack. He clutched at the big pot as it rolled from the rack, stared at it a moment and then picked up the frying pan with his free hand. He took a deep breath and stepped towards the tent.

The cat hissed, bared its teeth and braced itself for a leap at Tim's throat.

And Tim threw his arms wide and brought the frying pan and the big pot together with a shuddering clang.

The cat's savage hiss suddenly became a shriek of fright. The leap was now a fumbling retreat behind the sack.

Tim shouted in triumph and banged the pot and the pan together again and again, until the cat clawed under the rear wall of the tent in panic. He ran after the cat until it disappeared in the branches of the trees and he could hear clapping behind him.

The men were standing under a tree, laughing and applauding as if the Zeehan Military Band had just gone by. Oskar was bright red and spluttering, Straw leant weakly against the tree, Silent Eddy shook his head slowly. And Larry stepped forward with a broad smile.

'Maybe, kid,' he said. 'Maybe.'

That night they were calling Tim 'Tiger'.

# 7

# The Giant

In the days after the tiger Tim felt that the forest was
changing. In the camp Oskar accused Tim of feeding the
rivermen with tiger meat, but he was laughing. Straw
stopped protecting him from Larry because Larry was
finally leaving him alone. Even Silent Eddy started looking
at him with interest, as if he had just walked out of the
forest.

And out of the camp the trees and the river began to
open up, showing Tim a thousand quiet secrets.

Tim found seven small fungus umbrellas on a dead
trunk, placed so a drop of rain would trickle slowly in
seven steps from the first to the last. He found moss
growing an inch tall like a tiny forest in the cleft of a
rock; a discarded snake skin dangling from a branch;
lichens forming a garland of frost, tangled yellow threads
and curled orange mock flowers around a stump. He
would look down and see three determined ants carrying
the carcass of a spider, or a rush of grey, scuttling slaters
from a disturbed rock. A single strand of web swayed all
the way across a clearing, swooping from a distant wattle
to a brown bearded fern, flashing in the sun like the cable
of some great bridge.

But Tim's favourite spot was the rock on the river.

He could pick up a handful of water-worn shingles,
turn them in his fingers so they gleamed like black and
brown jewels, then skim them across the bubbling river

to the other bank. He would sit on the rock with his block in his hands and watch the mist slowly withdraw its long fingers from the blue morning forest. The currawong, a large black bird with cunning in its yellow eye, usually joined him in the first hour for breakfast scraps. He talked once to the currawong, as if it were Jean, about home and Ian, but he felt like a lonely little boy talking to a stupid bird, and stopped. He would look for the platypus, but it spent most of its time on the bottom chasing dinner. He relaxed, carved shavings from the block and allowed himself to think of Dad.

At first the pain was still there but there were too many good things to remember to stop now. Like the time the swimming dam had collapsed, dumping them in the water and covering them with black mud. And they just couldn't stop laughing. Then Dad had tried Tim's idea of sassafras stakes and it had worked. There was the time the owner of the Blood House watered the beer until Dad began to dig for silver right outside the pub's front door. And when a family picnic was trapped in a cave by a flash flood and they had entertained a damp wombat with six hours of song.

And when Dad had staggered from the surf around the wreck, shaken himself like a dog and started tearing at well-boiled mutton-bird leg.

'Couldn't get her,' he had said, nodding at the carved mermaid at the tilted bow of the wreck. 'A pity, but she wants to stay with her ship.'

Tim had laughed. 'It's only a piece of wood.'

'Hah!' Dad waved the mutton-bird leg at the figurehead. 'Look at her, swimming in the surf with her hair curling back over her shoulders and her mouth open, laughing. She's been to Shanghai, London and Naples. Maybe round Cape Horn to Rio and New York. Piece of wood? Can you imagine the sights she's seen?'

Tim turned from the block he was shaping and frowned.

Dad had these funny moments sometimes, like a kid in

the lolly shop, like when he talked about a waterfall in the heart of the wilderness, a waterfall so huge it shook mountains . . . .

Tim looked at the wilderness he was now accepting as easily as the dead mines of Zeehan, at the water curling from a near bend.

How close was the waterfall now?

'Your Dad still troubling you?'

Tim turned and saw Straw standing gloomily behind him.

'No.' Tim rubbed the block. 'Not much. Are we going to see the Thunderer?'

'Thunderer? Oh, your Dad's waterfall. I don't think so. We got a lot of work to do here.'

'Oh.' Just for a moment he thought of shouting, 'What about the promise?' but it had been made by Larry, not Straw, it had been made to Dad, not Tim, and it had never been a promise—just a 'maybe'. The Thunderer might as well never have existed. 'That why you look like you lost something?' he said.

Straw winced and shook his head. 'We are going to bring the big tree down. I guess that's why. But you might as well watch.'

Tim put the block away and followed Straw along the muddy trail to the first clearing quickly, stepping round puddles and the dying brush dug out by the dragging of the logs, then up a steepening slope. Their trail was marked by yellowing stumps and holes in the forest roof.

'Why don't you want to chop this tree down?' asked Tim.

'Ah, it's old. I would've liked to leave it so it gets older. But if we leave it the next mob gets it. You can't win.'

The slope levelled off and the track narrowed and roughened. Almost all the trees by the trail wore rope scars on their downhill side. Finally the mud gave way to a track of worn and sometimes broken branches. The straight sticks Tim had been asked to chop were now part of a corduroy path, looking a little like a jungle suspension bridge collapsed on the forest floor. Tim strode over the clattering track for fifty yards and stopped before the tree.

It was big. If he and Straw stood on opposite sides of the trunk they could touch each other's fingertips, but only just. It soared straight up for seventy feet before its lowest branch and there were forty more feet of light foliage.

'How old?' Tim said.

'About a thousand years.' Straw picked up an axe from a nearby stump and walked to Larry and the tree.

Tim decided right off that he would not count rings this time. Then he wondered how long a thousand years was. Older than Captain Cook? Everything's older than Captain Cook.

Older than the Great Plague.

Larry took off his waistcoat, worked his feet into the ground, looked over his shoulder at the corduroy track and swung his big axe at the tree, burying the blade in the bark. Straw swung an instant later, springing a great slab of lemon wood from the trunk and releasing Larry's axe to strike again. The two men worked together with the precision of an old clock, both swinging back and striking almost together, as if Straw knew exactly where Larry was going to strike. Swing tic toc, swing tic toc.

Older than Francis Drake.

Tim watched the crown of the tree scratching at the drifting clouds.

'They're good, eh lad?' Silent Eddy said. He was sharpening the saw.

Older than Columbus.

Swing tic toc.

'Just keep out of the way, boy.' Oskar nodded at Tim and walked towards the tree.

Swing tic.

Larry stepped back from the trunk onto the carpet of

108

fresh chips, leaving a wide gash, deep enough to reach the heart of the tree.

Older than the Crusaders.

'Come, Eddy,' Oskar said. 'Sometime you are expected to work.'

Silent Eddy gestured in disgust, but he carried the long saw to the back of the tree. The two men began to saw toward the gash but from a higher spot on the trunk.

Older than Robin Hood.

The chain, the tackle, and spare axes were carried past the tree, behind Oskar and Eddy on the saw. Ten minutes later the tree began to creak.

Older than the Battle of Hastings, 1066. About as old as William the Conqueror.

Oskar and Eddy looked at each other, quickly withdrew the saw and hurried back to the others. Tim watched the crown of the tree. It was still scratching the sky.

But the creaking increased and became a savage squeal as the wood at the heart of the trunk was slowly torn apart. A cloud passed over the tree, then the tip followed the cloud and overtook it. The tree cracked, rolled a little on its stump and crashed down into the forest. It splintered a tall blackwood tree, snapped the stump of a young celery-top pine six feet from the ground, and brought a shriek from a few birds.

'Nice job,' Larry said. The rivermen picked up their axes and móved along the trunk toward the branches.

'Can I help?' Tim said brightly.

Larry stopped and looked sideways. 'Help what?'

'Trim the tree. I am getting good with the small axe now.'

'Well—'

'Give him a go, Larry,' Straw said. 'You want to make him a riverman, he's got to get the hang of it.'

'Ah, go on.' Larry jerked a thumb at the trunk and resumed work.

Tim leapt onto the trunk eagerly and chopped at a thick

branch, watching the wood chips fly, breathing in the fresh sap scent. Suddenly he was no more the camp boy but a young axeman, pirate hunter and rugged explorer. Larry wanted him as part of the team!

Then Tim jammed his axe-head in the wood. He pulled, levered and kicked the handle; when the axe came free he staggered backwards under Larry's descending axe. Larry pulled back the blade in mid swing but he clipped Tim's handle.

'What the hell are you doing!' Larry's face was white and he was trembling.

'Take it easy, Larry,' Straw said.

'Oh, no, not this time.' Larry shook his axe at Straw. 'You want to go to Jean and tell her how he lost a leg? Eh?'

Straw fiddled with his axe.

Larry nodded at Tim and said: 'Go cook something.'

Tim walked back to his rock and threw pebbles into the river.

\* \* \*

For the next few days Tim saw as little of the tree and Larry as he could. He carried tea and damper to the rivermen at lunchtime, glanced at what they had done and returned to his camp and his rock, wishing he was round the next bend upsteam. And the next. And the next.

The biggest branches were brought to the river and branded, and the trunk was cut into five logs. The metal shoe was fitted to the first log as ropes and pulleys were connected to trees on either side to treble the men's strength, but it took a day and a half to move the log to the river—even with the corduroy track. The second, third and fourth logs were all heavier and took far longer, the fourth log taking two and a half days. Then it rained.

It poured for three days, penning Tim and the men in the two tents with very little to do. Tempers became so frayed that Tim spent an hour of the third day on his rock, drenched and trying to see across the river. But on the fourth day the sky cleared and Larry rubbed his hands and said: 'Well, now we've got greasy tracks. Be finished in no time at all.'

Two hours later Tim heard the scream.

He was filling a billy by the river when the hollow shriek of a man in agony burst from the forest, loud enough to cause Tim to stumble on the rock but distant enough to waver in the breeze. The scream stopped as suddenly as it started, but the sound kept spreading across the valley as a desperate echo. Tim stood as something big began to slide heavily through the trees, snapping branches, tearing at trunks, squealing angrily as it accelerated. It stopped in a splintering crash.

Tim walked shakily back to the silent camp, staring in the direction of the sounds but uncertain of what to do. He was still trying to decide when Larry strode from the forest with Oskar slumped in his arms like a huge rag doll.

''Aven't you got some water boiling, kid? Couldn't you hear?'

Straw and Eddy had collected sawdust at the stump of the big tree and arrived at the camp at the same time as Tim. Eddy knelt beside Oskar and started cutting his bloody right boot from his foot. Oskar looked light green, but he was breathing.

Tim lifted his eyes from Oskar to Straw.

'It got away,' Straw said. 'We were moving ropes about and then the last log started to slide downhill on the mud. Oskar would have made it, but he tripped.'

'We'll never shift the log now,' Larry said.

Straw squatted beside Eddy, watching him pack the foot in sawdust. 'What's it like?'

Eddy shrugged. 'Ankle's crushed.' He began to bandage the foot gently but firmly. 'But the Huon sawdust might save the foot 'til I get him back to Strahan.'

111

'Okay,' Larry sighed. 'D'you want help over Big Fall?'

'Nah. I may just push him in and watch.' But Eddy was smiling.

\* \* \*

Next morning one of the tents was taken down and loaded into a punt with Oskar and some food.

Oskar, grey-faced, shook hands with Larry and Straw and looked at Tim as if he could not make up his mind. 'Ah . . . you're not a real bad boy. Look after yourself.'

Silent Eddy snorted as he pushed off the punt and stepped into it. He looked briefly at Tim and almost smiled before drifting round a bend.

Larry walked back to the log, buried deeply in a clay bank with a trail of broken vines and brush behind it. He kicked it.

'Maybe we should've gone with them, Straw. We can't do anything now.'

Straw looked at Tim as if he was trying to remember something. Then he smiled. 'Oh, I don't know.'

'You got some half-baked ideas?'

'We could always go upstream, see what we can see.'

Tim blinked.

'What for?' Larry said blankly.

'See where the trees are for next time. Maybe prepare a couple for the floods.'

'Suppose we could do that—'

'Maybe even get into Deception Gorge far enough to see that waterfall. Your brother's "Thunderer".'

Larry turned to Tim and frowned. 'Maybe.'

Straw bent forward to scratch his knee and murmured to Tim, 'Someone's got to win something, sometime.'

# 8

# Deception Gorge

The punt quivered under Tim's hands as he stepped aboard. Rushing brown water exploded against the blunt bow, stinging his face with cold spray, and Larry shouted at Straw as both men groped for their oars. They slid from the bank, bucketed in the current and spun for a perilous handful of seconds until the oar blades bit into the river.

Tim had forgotten the pounding tension of the old battle with the river, and took a last wistful look at the quiet piece of wilderness that he had almost made his home. He could see where the tents had been, the tree marked by the tiger, his rock, even his currawong . . . . Then the bank curled round a bend. There was nothing left but the river.

He sat in the punt, watching the river buck and foam past as the scoured banks moved toward each other, and he began to grin. Already the river was narrowing, running faster, beginning to roar. Dad's country.

Soon he could see white water far ahead.

'Double Fall,' Straw panted. 'Try to get as close as we can?'

Larry nodded, exchanged his oar for a pole and stood in the punt.

Straw rowed hard with both oars, while Larry pulled the pole back to lever the punt into the bucking water.

Soon Straw was pushing his oars against water-carved boulders and Tim pushed the punt off the rocks.

'Now, Tim!' Larry yelled over the roar.

Tim turned in confusion for a moment and saw a tongue of rock almost under the punt's bow. He grabbed the bow rope, leapt for the rock and threw a loop over a boulder before the punt pulled back. Straw landed beside him, patted him on the shoulder and pulled the punt onto the rock.

'I did all right, didn't I?' shouted Tim.

Larry ignored him. 'Straw, take bow rope ahead.' He was bellowing. 'I'll put the punt into the rapid.'

Straw uncoiled the rope as he climbed beside a foaming channel of wild water and rocks. He stopped twenty feet away, passed the rope across his back and braced his legs. 'Okay!' he shouted.

'What do I do?' Tim said.

'Keep out of the way.'

Tim felt a touch of anger. Still a schoolboy. No matter what.

Larry flipped Tim's loop off the boulder, allowing the punt to slide back into the foam until Straw anchored it. Now boulders and a rock ledge lay between the punt and Straw. The two men couldn't shout to each other now and Larry had to push the punt sideways into the rushing water to move it. They fought the bucking punt and the rapids for forty minutes to ease it past the first fall, and a further twenty minutes to clear the entire stretch of rapids. They fell into the punt, panting, dripping, as Tim rowed them across a placid stretch of red tinged water to a beach of fine gravel for lunch.

That was how they travelled for the next few days. They would row and pole until the shallow rapids became too fast, then they would get out and wade. They would carry the punt over smooth grey rocks, with Tim scrambling beside them, and pull the punt through white rapids on a rope. They only trusted Tim with the oars on stretches of water smooth enough to reflect the sky. The river coiled, hissed and roared as the green mountains in the north slid slowly nearer.

Each day the men fought the rapids until mid-afternoon, camped where the river flowed quietly and Tim cooked a meal. Larry would walk off and search for any Huon pines, Straw would swim slowly in the river and Tim would find a spot to call his own.

He squatted on a rocky outcrop above the river a bend from the camp and watched the spray hang part of a rainbow over the water. He smiled as the afternoon warmed the river valley and thought this was the place that Dad was going to bring him. You could cast a line into the rushing shallows from this mossy rock all day and live off the mountain trout; you could pan for gold by that gravelly bank and you just might catch a grain or two. You could walk into the misty blue forest for a week and you would never find a sign that anyone had gone before you. Or you could look up at the mountains high above you, the gold cliff of Elliot range, the forested crown of Goodwyn's Peak, the flashing white quartzite of the distant Frenchman's Cap, and think of what it would be like if you were a bird. Yes, this was the place.

Except . . . .

A shadow fell across Tim's face.

'Great country, eh?' Straw smiled.

Tim shrugged.

'What's up?'

'He's not here.'

Straw nodded and squatted beside Tim. 'Yeah. I used to think what a pity it was that Isabel—my daughter— couldn't see any of this. I still do, but it is not quite so bad for Albert.'

Tim looked up sharply.

'He knew all this was here, all the mountains, the river, the forest, and that is almost as important as being here. Isabel never knew.'

115

Tim suddenly shouted in pain.

Straw smiled and flicked a heavy March fly from Tim's arm. 'Maybe just knowing is better than being here, eh? No getting rained upon, being nibbled, frozen, tired, chased by tigers—'

Tim smiled a little.

But Tim carved his block of Huon until dark fell, slowly now because it was beginning to look like something.

* * *

Next day they turned from Elliot Range and Straw pointed at a sagging landing on the west bank. 'Know where that leads, Tim?'

Tim was surprised to see any sign of people this far into the wilderness. 'No.'

'There's a track of sorts. Leads right to that hut we were at on the Gordon.'

'The Gordon?' That was weeks and weeks ago. It could not be.

'Way over there, the Gordon has been flowing north. The Franklin flows south to catch it. Some odd rivermen lug their punts over the track to save time.'

The next day they battled rapids to reach and pass the Jane River. They rowed up a broad, smooth stretch of water and camped at the edge of a basin, but the river was becoming faster and wilder.

The river sluiced over white limestone boulders carved into strange shapes and dyed red by the water. They passed under a cave that towered over the river like an emperor's throne and thin trees leaned over the water from clusters of boulders.

The next day they carried the punt and their stores beside a staircase of three foot drops in the river. They were all exhausted, but both men rowed toward a narrow pass through a grey rock cliff.

'This is it,' Straw said.

'Deception Gorge?' Tim leaned forward in the boat. 'I can hear water falling.'

'It's the beginning. Rock Island Bend.'

'All right. Keep to one side. We'll see if we can make it.'

Straw and Larry rowed steadily towards the cleft, but accelerated as the water whitened and seethed past them. From the rear of the punt Tim saw a high slab of rock separated from both sides of the cleft with still water on one side, swirling water on the other. The punt slowed in the rush and stopped, despite the oars flailing the water. Tim saw the punt was being turned, then swept round so the men were rowing desperately in the wrong direction.

'Stop!' he shouted.

Straw stopped and blinked and Larry heaved the boat round.

'Again!' Larry urged Straw into action.

'Tim, point us through,' Straw panted. 'Keep pointing.'

Larry looked annoyed but rowed to keep Tim's raised arm between him and Straw. They cut through several spinning eddies and passed a huge rock just under the surface but they turned where the river turned and passed the cleft in the rock.

Ahead a stream of water arched out from the west wall to explode near some rapids battering past a long set of boulders. Tim was expecting a river-wide waterfall with a huge drop. He was disappointed.

'This time we carry the punt, okay?' Larry said.

They were now in a low slit, a silver ribbon with great green mountains pushing in from either side. They camped on a rock ledge in a quiet stretch of river, but Straw noticed that the winter flood mark was twenty feet above the camp.

Larry came back from his daily hunt for logs tired and bad-tempered. 'I shouldn'a been talked into coming up here,' he said. 'There's nothing here. Or if there is, it's not worth cutting down.'

117

'We've only started.'

'You're just like the kid. You only want to see the waterfall.'

'I want to see if we can get through—'

'Just mad.'

But they moved further into the gorge. Waterfalls dropped from high clefts on sheer walls, mist flowed heavily over the water until the sun rose enough to throw warmth and light into the gorge. Most of the time the punt was out of the water, being manhandled past twisting rapids and over cataracts.

In mid-afternoon the punt was launched into a broad pool and Tim rowed slowly toward a narrow gorge with Larry and Straw sprawled at the ends of the boat. Deep in the gorge Tim could see a great log lying across the river, with water bubbling under it. He was wondering how they would get the punt over the log when he heard a low rumble, as if a distant mountain was moving.

'What's that?' Tim said. But he knew. He looked around him, at the river and the rearing green walls blocking the sky. He could smell the mists of the Thunderer.

'Ah, we'll find out tomorrow,' said Straw.

'What's the point?' Larry muttered. 'There's no Huon here.'

'But there is!' Tim dropped an oar and pointed.

# 9

# Walker's Tree

For a moment there was a small halo of light green high on the valley wall, then the punt bobbed and it disappeared.

'There's nothing there,' muttered Larry.

'I saw something. Biggie too,' Straw said. 'Backpaddle a little, Tim.'

Tim pushed on the oars, trying to move the stern along the lazy wrinkle it had left in the water a few seconds ago.

'There it is.' Straw pointed.

'It's a long way up.'

A steep forested valley twisted down to the pool, following a small creek as it bounced and bubbled into the still water. On the northern slope big trees, sassafras, myrtle, blackwood, King Billy pines, jostled each other, stood on each other's shoulders and swayed in the afternoon breeze. And a spray of light green reached from behind a giant celery top pine to touch the sky.

'Look at the slope,' Straw said, sounding a little like a man selling his dog, saying all the right things but hoping the dog won't be sold anyway. 'Fell it and it will slide all the way to the valley bottom. Just brand it and wait for the floods. That tree might be worth the trip by itself.'

'We going to see it?' said Tim.

Larry sighed. 'Tomorrow.'

That night the men and Tim lay beside the quiet yellow

119

glow of a fire, watching the stars roll slowly from black peak to dark cliff with the moon shimmering in the still pool. Tim carved the last main seams in his Huon block while he listened to the distant thunder of the river.

It would be okay to stay here forever, Tim thought drowsily. He looked at the glittering river surging under the log deep in the gorge and remembered Dad's wreck. With that wooden mermaid at the bow, thrusting into the creaming surf and laughing . . . .

Tim sat up. But this was far better than the wreck. This is all of what Dad wanted to see and feel.

Tim looked at the log for a long time and began to smile.

Perhaps, in a way, he still would.

Next morning Larry and Straw picked up their axes and a couple of tins of herring and tomato sauce from the punt while Tim shoved last night's damper and his carved block in a hessian bag. They walked to where the small creek cascaded into the glinting pool and began to climb.

Sometime later Tim stopped, panting, on a rock and looked back at the bright ribbon of the river. He could see the turbulent rapids they had fought so hard to pass yesterday and the great black log that looked even more like the wreck. Beyond the log the river threaded through dark canyons, still heavy with mist. Waiting.

He turned and realized he was alone. He hurried after Larry and Straw, climbing an entangled ridge which dipped away from the river. He was about to shout for help when he ran into Straw's back.

'—never seen anything like this,' Straw was saying.

'It's a great ugly hulk, isn't it? No good to anyone.'

The tree Tim had seen from the river now looked like a giant celery plant. Four huge branches, as thick as mature trees, reared from the main trunk no more than a yard from the ground. The main trunk split into two at Larry's height. The branches carried so much debris, trunks, parts of fallen trees, it looked like it had been in a flood. It was the ugliest tree Tim had ever seen.

Straw walked over to the trunk and spread his arms across it, as if he was going to pull it out. But five Straws, fingertip to fingertip, could not get round that trunk.

He paced round the tree, stared up through the foliage and came back. 'You aren't going to cut that tree down, Larry.'

'Sure, sure. Let's have a bit of damper.'

'No, I mean it this time, Larry. You're not going to take that tree. Ever.'

'Okay, okay son. It's all yours.'

'Oh.' Straw was building up for a long, hot row and this sudden surrender confused him. 'Okay. Fine.'

Larry suddenly laughed. 'I can't use it, Straw. Look at that drop. If we cut the tree, it wouldn't slide—it would smash itself to pieces on the rocks down there. Even if it survived the drop no flood would carry it down to the river. And if it somehow got to the Franklin the rapids would smash it to matchwood before it got to the Gordon. On top of that, you'd be lucky to get fifty feet of straight timber. You can have this one.'

Straw shook his head. 'No, I didn't find it. It's Tim's tree. What are you going to call it, Tim?'

Tim looked at Straw with a single cunning eye. 'Name it? Name a tree?'

'You have no idea what you've found, have you?'

Tim shrugged. 'It's a tree.'

'It's a worthless tree,' Larry said.

'Good. Then it might just keep on growing.'

'What's so special about it?' said Tim.

'How old do you think it is?'

'A thousand years. I dunno.'

'That was the big tree that almost killed Oskar. That was taller, but look at the thickness of the trunk.' Straw squatted and cleared a broad patch of earth. He drew with a stick the lumpy circle of the ugly tree, as if cut through

121

the trunk. He drew a smaller circle inside the lumpy circle like a fat doughnut. 'That much smaller.'

Older than a thousand years? Nothing can be that old. Tim looked back at the scarred limbs of the tree, carrying a small forest of dead timber. Well, perhaps this tree could.

'What's the oldest thing—the oldest piece of history you can think of?'

'Um, Alfred the Great, I suppose,' Tim shrugged.

'Here.' Straw poked at the lumpy circle, no more than a quarter of the way toward the centre. 'Only twelve hundred years ago, you're not really trying.'

'The Romans.'

Straw moved his stick half way to the centre. 'That's a little better. The start of the Republic of Rome?'

'The Greeks.' Tim was struggling.

The stick moved towards the centre, but not far.

'Ah, come on Straw.' Larry was shaking his head.

'The Pyramids.' Tim was determined to move that stick to the centre if he had to shovel out all the dusty pages from his old history books.

The stick rolled across centuries, but stopped almost an inch from the centre. 'That gives you the Great Pyramid, about 2600 BC. The tree is older than that.'

'What are you trying to pull, Straw?' Larry was annoyed. 'How old do you think this ragged tree *is*?'

'Well—' Straw hesitated and tugged at his ear. 'Larry, you know we've brought in trees a thousand years old so often nobody notices. We've brought in a two thousand year tree and we've seen stumps of three thousand year trees. They were smaller, far smaller across than this.'

'C'mon, Straw—'

'Just look at the size of the trunk, Larry. I don't know when a Huon pine has to die of old age, nobody does. Perhaps they never die that way, they get killed by fire, flood, lightning, and by us—'

'How old, Straw?'

'I think five thousand years, Larry.'

Larry started to smile, then he saw that Straw was not joking. 'Give me that again.'

'Five thousand years. About as long as people have been doing things.'

Tim stared at the tree. He tried to understand the figure, but Straw might as well have said 'fifty thousand years'. It was beyond his imagination.

Straw smiled at him. 'It means that tree is a book on us. When it pushed a shoot out of the earth, people in Europe still had stone-tipped spears. But when it was little more than a sapling the Egyptians were building pyramids and cities of stone. By the time it had reached its full height Moses and the Hebrews had left Egypt and the Chinese had learnt to write. Maybe it endured a drought when Ghengis Khan rolled his armies toward China, sprouted a branch when Magellan sailed round the world. Everything that we've done is in the lines of that tree—Buddha, Da Vinci, Galileo, Shakespeare, Magellan, they're all there. And that tree is still growing with us, marking everything we do.'

Tim walked slowly round the tree, running his fingers over the rough bark. It wasn't a tree, it was more than that. A monument, but it was alive. Maybe more important than a dozen waterfalls. He ducked under a massive limb and looked down at the log stroked by flashing water, the wild gorges, the river threading through the silent wilderness. And smiled.

'Well, what're you going to call the tree, Tim?' Larry said with a rare grin. 'The World According To Straw?'

Tim walked back from the Huon pine and took his finely carved block of Huon from his hessian bag. 'I dunno,' he said. It didn't really matter.

'It's up to you,' Straw said.

Tim ran his fingers over his carving, feeling the hollows, the ridges, the curl in the lemon wood, the features that had brought the block to life. He looked at the ancient tree, set deep in the rock of a mountain and spreading to become a forest on a single root.

'Can I call it Walker's Tree?' he said.

# 10

# Flood

The weather began to change on the way back to the river. The fluffy cumulus clouds of the morning were pushed aside by thin mare's-tails high in the sky and a light north wind tossed the tree tops in the gorge.

'Bit of rain,' said Larry.

'Do you want to go on?'

'Ah, we'll give it a go. When even the kid finds special trees there has to be something for us old blokes.'

Tim looked back for a moment but he could not see the tree any more. Now he was going to see the Thunderer, but it was too late to undo what had been done. He shrugged and walked on.

By the time they reached the river a thick, even film of cloud had spread over the sky. The wind had dropped completely, leaving the pool a motionless, grey picture of the sky. Soft, heavy banks of cloud had drifted around the peaks of the mountains and humped into the backs of bad tempered hogs.

'Better move the tent up the slope,' Straw said.

'And the punt. Get the fire going, Tim.'

A breath of air rippled across the pond, followed by a few drops of rain.

Tim built the fire high up the bank as Straw rigged the fly over him. The rain grew into a steady drizzle, heavy rain, a downpour. They ate corned beef and onion inside the tent while the fly bucked wildly against the guys and sleeting rain drowned the fire.

Tim pressed his eye to the trembling tent flap to see slopes of trees sway and toss as a cold blast of wind tore down the gorge. He did not look out of the tent any more, but went to sleep listening to thunder rolling down the mountains.

Next morning the rain and the wind had stopped, but the pool had become a small lake and the roar from the river seemed to have moved closer.

'We wait until it goes down?' said Straw.

Larry shook his head. 'It's better now than before. Faster, but with less rocks. We'll have a look over that log.'

Before, the log had stretched from one side of the gorge to the other, dry on top like a dam wall with the river shouldering through a net of branches and debris underneath. Now the river slid easily over the top and dropped six feet to a storm of brown foam. With Larry and Straw rowing very fast, Tim crouched in the bow with rope in his hand and waited as the punt slowly approached the log. It now looked like a log in a river, never a ship in the sea.

Tim heard a heavy, creaking sound.

He looked around, saw nothing but the rocks and swirling foam. He shrugged and concentrated on the safe rock inching toward him. He jumped for the rock and held the punt while Larry shipped the oar and landed beside him.

'Now let's see what we got—'

Something massive was grinding against stone.

Larry was staring at the log, the trunk of a huge blackwood tree, five feet across with a foot of brown water sliding over the top. And it was moving.

'Straw!' Larry shouted and turned.

The boulder pinning the log splintered with a small crack. The log rolled free, hurling a curling wave at Tim

126

and the punt. Straw half-stood, staring at the log. Larry snatched the rope from Tim and threw it back in the punt. A wall of water swept the punt from the log and Straw dived for the seats. Larry was reaching for Tim when the wave hit them both.

Tim was tumbled, bounced and rolled, cold, blinded and alone. Something wrenched at his left ankle, scraped his nose and shoved him hard in the back. He seemed to be at the bottom of the river, moving very fast. The river rolled him, tore at him and somersaulted him to the surface.

He gasped and cleared his eyes. He saw the log surging through the water beside him and the punt twisting far ahead. He thought he could see Straw's head in the stern of the punt, but the head wasn't moving. There was no sign of Larry and the rush of water was carrying Tim through and out of the pool.

He tried to swim across the white water and away from the log, but the river swept him towards the rocky rapids they had fought past two days ago. He was able to get his feet in front of him as he dropped into a rocky chute with the log behind him.

He looked back, thought, oh hell, and was corkscrewed past boulders, ledges, propped branches and over white stones, trying to go faster than the water as the great log pounded against the boulders close behind him. But after a long race down the rapids he looked back and glimpsed the log jammed against a rock again.

Then the river lost its bottom.

For a second time he was in the air, part of a heavy curve of water hanging from a lip of black rock. The air became water, dark water, and he was being tumbled with bubbles swirling about him. He tried to swim to the surface but he was being spun back down, again and again. He lost his sense of direction, his lungs became hot and his throat fought desperately to breathe.

127

He clawed for help, for anything, and he began to scream.

Something caught him by the hair and took him down, down against his fighting body, until his hands were thrashing at gravel. Then the river was moving him on again. The water was lighter, whiter and he was gasping air.

Someone was dragging him out of the water and across a rock. It was over, and he began to cough his lungs clear.

When he opened his eyes Larry was sitting on a rock, shaking his head as if to get rid of the water on his face.

'Thanks, Larry.'

'You should have swum down. Remember? Can you see Straw?'

Tim looked up and down the river. He shook his head.

'Well?' Larry was looking intently at his left hand while he knuckled his eyes with his right.

'No. I can't see him.' Something was wrong. Tim got to his feet, staggered and fell.

'What's wrong, lad?'

'My foot. Something's broke.'

'Jesus. That's all we need. Straw can't come back for us.'

'He's okay, then?'

'He'll be right. Saw him moving in the punt. But he'd lost his oars. Even with them he can't come back against the rapids for us.'

'Oh. Then we can follow him, can't we?'

'What, with you like that? No, you can't follow the Franklin on foot, kid. And we don't know where he's made it to the bank. If he's made it to the bank.'

Larry turned to Tim. He had an ugly purpling gash on his right temple. 'We're in a bit of trouble, boy. There's safety and some help just a mountain or so away, but it's too far for us.'

128

Tim swallowed. 'Maybe you could go and get help. I'll be all right while you're gone.'

'Maybe you'd be all right, lad, but it doesn't matter.'

'Why?' But Tim saw the answer in Larry's face before he spoke.

'I can't see.'

# 11

# Into the Dark . . .

'What's wrong?' It was no more than a whisper.

'I don't know, boy.' He breathed heavily, as if he was trying to remember something. 'I think I was hit getting us out of the river. My head wants to drop off. I can't see anything at all.'

Tim could hear a faint tremble in Larry's voice—that was more frightening than the blindness itself. Like a mountain turning to mud and slithering away. 'What do we do?'

'Take it easy, boy.' Larry stared through Tim and patted the air. 'It may go away. Go and see if there's anything from the punt we can use. I want to think.'

Tim started to remind Larry that he couldn't go, his foot was broken, then he stopped. He pulled himself to his good foot and hauled himself away, moving from rock to rock. He found one of the punt's oars and leaned on it until the throbbing in his foot eased.

There was nothing else. Larry was sitting hunched beside the cascading river with those mountains of blue-green forest towering round him and no shelter, no food. They were hopelessly trapped, as if they had been shoved into a cage and left to die. Even if Straw was still in the punt, even if he had been able to get it to the bank with one or no oars, even if he could get a new pole from the forest and ride the rapids, how long would it take him to get help and come back?

Too long. Much too long.

But Larry was just sitting by the river trying to think of a way out, as if it was all no worse than a Chinese puzzle. As if there *had* to be a way out.

Tim turned from the river and looked up at the forest, marching down from a grey barrier of cloud, tree upon tree upon tree, with no space at all between them. After a while he went back to Larry.

'Anything?' said Larry to the sound of Tim panting.

'Just an oar. I been thinking—'

'We all have, boy. It's no good.'

'I'm pretty light.'

'Eh? so?'

'Maybe you can carry me?'

'Kid, I still can't see.'

'I got eyes.'

Larry was silent, but he frowned.

'I can tell you where to go.'

And then Larry laughed. 'I bet you can, kid.'

'It's worth trying, isn't it?'

'It's the stupidest idea I ever heard. You'd break our necks in ten steps.'

'Oh.'

Larry sat in silence and listened to the water for a while. Then he sighed and pushed himself unsteadily to his feet. 'I guess we'll have to give it a go.'

He helped Tim onto his back, took the oar and leant on it. 'Right, kid, tell me what you can see.'

'Well, we're on the west bank of the river, and there's rapids upstream and there's a small waterfall downstream, close—'

'Forget about the river. We're leaving it. What about the bush? Can you see the Elliot range?'

'No. The forest is thick and steep here.'

'Get us into the forest the easiest way you can. We've got to go up, west then south. Okay, here we go.'

Larry shuffled forward toward the sound of the waterfall

131

and Tim began steering the big man. 'There's a rock in front, slopes left, branch high as your knee—higher, higher—loose stones, go right, go up, there's a puddle left—'

Their first fall split them apart over a rock and Tim shouted in pain. Larry apologized for slipping and Tim apologized for yelling, and they moved slowly from the river.

For a while they climbed moss-green rocks by the waterfall, Larry throwing away the oar to clutch at feeder roots and jam his feet against thin trees and rotting logs. Tim parted ferns before Larry's head and bit back shouts when Larry forced his injured foot against the rocks. They seemed to be climbing straight up for a long time and Larry stopped for a breather as rain swept over them.

'You sure you know what you're doing?' Larry said.

'Yes. It gets better.' In fact, Tim was fast losing his grip of where they were. He found that with the desperate concentration in keeping Larry on his feet he could not plan where they were going. They were moving, and they were moving up from the river, but that was all he knew.

After a short break they climbed beside the waterfall until it became a cascade, then a creek. They crossed the creek and plunged into dense rain forest. The forest was like a great green cave now, deadening the waterfall to a dull mutter and the blasting rain to a gentle drip. They moved under manferns, between the lichen-scarred myrtle trunks and over a soft carpet of moss and peat. For a while they were climbing smoothly.

'Now we're getting somewhere,' said Larry.

'Stop,' said Tim heavily.

Larry stopped. 'What's up, kid?'

Before Tim was a tangled mass of thin branches, growing up, growing down, growing anywhere like a child's finger-painting. 'There's a mess of branches. We can't get through.

132

Larry walked cautiously forward and ran his fingers over one of the branches. He sighed and eased Tim from his back. 'Horizontal,' he said. 'Scrub that was put here to drive blokes mad.'

Tim knew it. The scrub grew more than twelve foot high before falling over because it couldn't support its crown. So the crown lay in the ground and put roots in the ground and more thin trunks grew up and fell over. And so it goes on. And on. Tim knew it, but he had never seen it like this before.

'Can we walk round?' asked Larry.

'I dunno. There's a lot of it.'

'We can't go through. Maybe we can go under. You crawl and I'll follow.'

Tim wriggled into the horizontal scrub and Larry barrelled along on his elbows and knees. He did not seem to need Tim's guidance, but their progress was slow. They were still deep in the scrub when night came.

Tim stopped in the darkness and groped vainly for a way out of a black cage. He was whimpering, shaking, as he began to thrash about under the scrub.

'Okay, okay.' Larry was shaking his shoulder. 'I'll lead for a bit.'

Larry slithered smoothly over Tim, rocked, and moved on ahead. Tim clutched grimly at Larry's disappearing boot. Half an hour later Larry reached back and prised Tim's fingers from his ankle.

'You can stand up now.'

Tim tried to grab Larry's foot again and realized that there was nothing in front of him or above him. He stood up, but for five minutes he could not stop trembling.

'Sorry,' he said. 'Sorry, sorry—'

'That's all right,' Larry said in a voice that was surprisingly gentle. 'You did fine. Find us a spot to sleep.'

Tim found a sheltered hollow where a tree had died and been ripped from the soil. The hollow was now filled with leaves and century-old peat. It was damp and probably had a few slaters and centipedes but it would do for the night.

They huddled in the hollow and Tim listened to the steady dripping of the forest.

Larry's not that bad, he thought. Even a little friendly.

When he has to be.

★ ★ ★

Tim woke shivering as the branches over his head swayed and clattered. Larry was looking at his hand.

'Can you see now?' Tim said, bright with hope.

'Nah, you're still the boss. But the head's not so bad. Maybe it's getting lighter. Get me a long root or a vine— and can you see something I can use as a pole?'

Larry knotted a loop of heavy vine before his belly to hold Tim's legs tight on his own hips. Now he had his arms free he could use the straight branch Tim had found to feel the ground before him.

'Now kid, it's up to you to stay mounted.'

'Gee up,' said Tim, and tried to smile.

Larry moved steadily up the slope, waving his staff as if he wanted to fight all the trees in the forest. Tim found that he didn't have to talk so much and he could plan their direction ten minutes ahead. The trees were becoming smaller, thinner and the slope was beginning to level off, but it was getting colder.

Larry barged through a bush and an icy wind streaked their faces. He stopped long enough to touch his face and tasted his fingers.

'Snow? Lovely, that is.'

He swung his staff, hit nothing and stepped out onto a brown grassy plain, glinting with frost and broad patches of snow. Suddenly the dripping forest was nothing more than tongues of stunted trees and bushes on the plain and green shadows on distant hills. To their right a bald mountain shouldered the grey cloud ceiling.

134

'We're out of the forest,' Tim said.

'A big flat place? Button grass? It has to be Western Plains. See the Elliot range?'

Tim compared the bald mountain with the bare cliff he had seen so much from the river. It had to be. 'Yup.'

'Okay. Now all you have to do is steer us at the peak. There's a track between us and it and the walk is from here is all downhill. We just might make it.'

Tim doubled his trousers under the cutting vine and tried to keep his throbbing foot from Larry's leg as they turned sideways to the wind and began to cross the plain. He thought of asking Larry if he could hop on his own but realized that he would fall constantly among the clumps of grass, Larry was almost walking fast and if they didn't get off this plain soon they would freeze. He shut up and clenched his hands to keep his blood moving.

After two hours of strengthening winds and stinging snow they staggered into the protection of trees in a shallow dip. Larry slipped the loop from Tim's legs and Tim fell heavily to the ground, unable to move to save himself. Tim was feeling sleepy

'What's up, boy?' Larry was groping for him.

'Tired—' murmured Tim. He relaxed and the snow felt warm in his face.

Suddenly Larry grabbed Tim's arms, stared wildly through him and slapped his face. 'C'mon, c'mon, c'mon!'

'Hey!' Tim rolled out of reach and his surprise was pushed aside by weeks of suppressed anger. 'What d'you think y'are? Try that again and I'll leave yer.'

Larry grinned as if this was fun and leapt at his voice.

Tim yelped and scrabbled away, his injured foot screaming at him. 'I mean it, I'll leave—' he shouted, as Larry caught him across the chest. The great ape's gone mad, he thought in fright. The river's knocked him silly.

'Who'll leave who? Eh? Eh?' Larry bellowed as he beat him all over his body. 'Who'll leave who now?'

# 12

# . . . And Out

Then it stopped.

Larry rocked back on his heels. 'You awake now?'

Tim rolled away and hunched tensely, panting and ready to hop wildly to safety.

'Well?'

'Yes.' No more than a low mumble.

'Okay,' Larry nodded. 'You can't go to sleep now. You'll die. A mate lost a hand after a blizzard out here. He couldn't keep the blood moving. Your blood moving?'

'Oh,' Tim said, and relaxed. He felt his fingers and toes tingling, his arms pulsing, and his face hot. 'That was it.'

Larry tilted his head, as if tasting Tim's words. 'Just that. Would you really have gone off on your own?'

Tim hesitated. 'Nah.'

'You were pretty mad, weren't you?'

Tim shrugged.

'Maybe I've been too hard on you, kid. I'm good only with rivers and trees and blokes. I don't know anything about kids. Not like Straw.' He opened and closed his hands. 'Well . . . sorry.'

Tim was actually embarrassed. He tried an odd smile, then realized Larry could not see his face and coughed. 'It was all right.'

And strangely enough, it was.

The snow stopped ten minutes later. They left the cluster of trees to cross the beginnings of a creek and a last stretch of plain. Then Tim suddenly straightened on Larry's back.

Larry stopped, the wind flogging his hair. 'You got a view?'

'I can see it all,' Tim said softly. 'Everything.'

To his right Tim could see the sun breaking through piled black cloud to give a small halo to the distant bay of Strahan. He could even imagine seeing the smoke from the Zeehan smelters coiling over his childhood country. There was the swimming dam, the fire brigade, the big school, the Gaiety Theatre, so far away and so long ago. What a little kid he had been then. But there was also Jean and Ian, and he would see them soon, see how they had changed.

On the rim of Strahan's bay there might be a train, too far to see, on the way to Queenstown. Maybe *Number Three*, the loco that once hurled a silly kid towards a smoking mine, the kid somehow thinking he was on a great adventure. But Dad was no longer in the mine. Not now.

Closer, Macquarie Harbour spread between the dark mountains, wind-wrinkled like an old sheet, and the Gordon river flowed quietly behind a forested slope. A great horse, pirates, a warm hut, all down there—and the hut must be found.

Tim looked up at the massive Elliot range straight ahead and streaming torn mist from its peak. He had lived round the range for so long that he knew it as well as Mount Zeehan. But there had been a world of difference. Mount Zeehan had been as friendly as a neighbourhood dog, you saw it every day from your backyard, and you had climbed it. The Elliot range reared out of the wilderness, changing with the weather, watching as you slowly fought past its face, mysterious and untouchable.

And to his left there was a shining stretch of the Franklin. Down there he had explored ancient forests, battled rapids, cooked for a bunch of irritable rivermen for more than a month, fought a tiger single-handed and found a tree older than Moses. And more, much more.

'Seen enough?' said Larry.

'Why did you bring me up the rivers?'

Larry boosted Tim over his shoulders and began to walk downhill. 'You don't believe I just brought you to cook, to earn money for Jean?'

'No. Not just for that.'

Larry nodded slowly. 'When Bert got it in the mine I just wanted to get lost in the bush for a while. I figured you might feel the same.'

'Thanks, Larry,' Tim said. He realized that he wanted to come back. If he got out this time.

They walked quickly off the button grass plain and descended quickly through the forest. Tim didn't have to say so much now as Larry was developing some sort of instinct and could feel his way faster than Tim could describe it. But Tim stopped Larry near the bottom of a valley.

'A kind of path,' he said.

'Lovely, mate. All we have to do now is walk home.'

Tim looked at the sky and at the long shadows on the hills. 'We're losing the sun.'

'Can you still see?'

'Oh, yeah.'

'Come on, Tim. Let's get to the convict's hut tonight. Get a fire going.'

'Sure.' Tim realized with a low shock that this was the first time Larry had called him by name.

Larry's pace increased as the roughly-cut track wound over and round hills and spurs, but rivulets constantly bubbled across and the track was marked by long, muddy puddles.

'Larry, you better slow down . . . I can't see much now, it's dark.'

'Okay.'

They moved more slowly and unsteadily as they both

138

became exhausted. Tim's foot felt like a block of hot iron, no longer a part of him. His legs were slowly being cut off by the vine and he was sure he could feel the blood running down his ankle. He had to whisper directions to Larry because his voice was gone. Larry was staggering down the track and he fell forward onto his knees three times in half a mile. Tim kept peering into the black for any sign of the path but it was slowly disappearing before him.

'Larry—'

Larry grunted.

'I've lost the track.'

'Jesus.'

They hung together, Larry leaning on the staff like a tired giant with a hump. They would have to sit down here, lie down here and forget about the hut . . . .

'Hang on.' Larry sniffed. 'There's wood smoke in the air.'

He took a step and slid into an icy creek, dragging Tim under. Tim fought clear and he and Larry crawled up the other side of the creek with Tim's legs locked around Larry's waist.

Then Tim came as close to shouting as he could. 'There's a light!'

He hauled himself back onto Larry's back and the big man was urged in a running stumble towards the flickering glow. The hut, with its little parade of pines, grew out of the forest mist.

Larry banged triumphantly on the wall.

'Who's there?' a sleepy voice called from the hut.

'Just a couple of old rivermen,' said Larry.

# Riverman

'And that's it,' said the old man.

Brian rested his chin on his knees and watched him digging carefully at the base of the tree. 'But what happened to Straw, Mr Walker? What happened to them all?'

Tim stopped digging and poured some water from his bottle into the hole he had dug. 'Well, Oskar got off with a limp, but he never came back to the rivers. Larry got his eyes back in a couple of days and we caught Straw sculling the punt down the Gordon with his remaining oar. The three of us spent a couple of years on the rivers, then the Great War broke us up.'

'Did you ever get to see the Thunderer?'

Tim was rubbing at part of the tree's root, but he looked down at the silver river winding back into the mountains. He shook his head.

'Too much trouble. Thirty years later the Morrison brothers got through Deception Gorge and it nearly killed them too. They didn't find any waterfalls up there, just rapids wild enough to shake a mountain. They don't call it Deception Gorge any more, just the Great Ravine with rapids like the Churn, Coruscades, Thunderush, the Cauldron.'

Tim shrugged. 'There's not much left now. Zeehan is still there, but my old house has gone and there's a great flat plain of wild grass where thousands of houses used to be. The smelter is gone, the railway is gone. They've put a road where the railway used to be between Zeehan and Strahan, Teekoophana has vanished and Three Quarter Mile Bridge has been destroyed by the King river. *Number Three* has been polished and painted and set up in Queenstown but she has nowhere to go. The mine has disappeared. The huge hill where the tunnel was has been eaten away to feed the smelters. Strahan shrunk away and there're no rivermen left.'

Tim used a handkerchief to polish the old wood. 'But the tree's still there. Your tree now, if you want it.'

Brian looked up at the six trunks and the centuries of debris carried by the massive branches. He thought about the age of the tree and he felt his neck prickling.

'What do you do with it?'

Tim shrugged. 'Not much, really. Worry about it. Make sure some damn fool doesn't build a road through it or build a house with it. Just keep it growing.'

Not a gift, a responsibility. 'Oh,' Brian said flatly.

Tim slapped his handkerchief away from the cleaned timber.

The tree had built a thumbnail of new wood around the carved block Tim had placed against the trunk seventy years ago. Seventy rings of fine wood marking time.

'That head?' Brian was shuffling away from decision. 'That why you came back?'

'M'dad's body was found in the mine with the others and buried in Queenstown cemetery. But that's only a body. I like to think of him being here, with the river below him. Hey, Dad?'

A man's head was set into the tree, a man with a pair of old square spectacles, cropped hair, a light scar across his right cheekbone and laugh wrinkles set around his mouth. He was looking across the valley, at a forest being tossed and swirled by a sudden wind, at a bald mountain trailing a long white cloud, at the river glinting in the sun. He had become part of the tree, part of the valley.

141

Like an old ship's figurehead, seeing the world.

'Well?' Tim said to Brian.

Brian smiled at the carved head and Albert Walker smiled back at him.

Some families have castles, business empires, yachts, or broad stretches of land. The Walker family have on trust an ugly old tree so deep in the wilderness very few people know it is there.

'I'll look after it,' said Brian.

## About the Author

Allan Baillie was born in Scotland in 1943, but has lived in Australia since he was seven years old. On leaving school he worked as a journalist and travelled extensively. He now lives in Sydney with his wife and two children and writes full time. He is the author of seven highly acclaimed novels for children, and a prize-winning picture book:

*Adrift* (Shortlisted for the 1985 Australian Children's Book of the Year Award, and winner of the 1983 Kathleen Fidler Award)

*Little Brother* (Highly commended in the 1986 Australian Children's Book of the Year Awards)

*Riverman* (Winner of the 1988 IBBY Honour Diploma [Australia] and shortlisted for the 1987 Australian Children's Book of the Year Award)

*Eagle Island*

*Megan's Star* (Shortlisted for the 1989 Australian Children's Book of the Year Award)

*Hero* (A Children's Book Council of Australia Notable Book 1991)

*The China Coin* (Shortlisted for the 1992 Guardian Children's Fiction Award and the 1992 SA Festival Literary Award)

*Drac and the Gremlin* (Winner of the 1989 Australian Picture Book of the Year Award)

# MORE GREAT READING FROM PUFFIN

☆☆☆☆☆☆☆☆☆☆☆☆☆☆☆☆☆☆☆☆☆☆☆☆☆☆☆☆

**Megan's Star**   Allan Baillie

Kel has rare powers and knows that Megan has them too. But as they explore their capabilities, Megan realises she must soon give up all she knows, for there will be no turning back.

*Shortlisted for the 1989 Australian Children's Book of the Year Award and the 1989 NSW Premier's Award.*

**Eagle Island**   Allan Baillie

When chance brings Col and Lew together on a lonely island in the Great Barrier Reef, their encounter turns into a deadly game of hide and seek.

**Hero**   Allan Baillie

The Hawkesbury River has broken its banks and the children must get home before the black water overwhelms the bridges. Four hours later they meet in dramatic and terrifying circumstances, and one of them will become a hero. But which one?

*A Children's Book Council of Australia Notable Book, 1991.*

**The China Coin**   Allan Baillie

Leah steps into China with her mother, loaded with her father's obsession about an ancient coin. But as they journey across this vast and bewildering land, they are drawn slowly towards the terror of Tiananmen Square ...

*Shortlisted for the 1992 Guardian Children's Fiction Award and the 1992 SA Festival Literary Award.*